CW00853245

"A fascinating and moving insight into the ..... of Malta during WW2 – seen through the eyes of a 21st century British school student."

Tom Palmer, award winning author of Armistice Runner and D-Day Dog.

"Gentle themes of friendship and family are carefully balanced with high drama. A thought-provoking tale with more than a hint of the supernatural."

Lesley Parr, award winning author of The Valley of Lost Secrets and When the War Came Home.

"Heartbreakingly sad, but also devilishly funny. Wings is a smashing read for everyone."

Huw aged 11.

"I think it's a wonderful book that makes you feel happy, sad and anxious."

Lola aged 10

"It's a very emotional book and you can learn how gruesome war is."

Nico aged 10

ON WINGS TO THE STARS

KATE POELS

Matador
Unit E2 Airfield Business Park
Harrison Road, Market Harborough
Leicestershire LE16 7UL
Tel: 0116 279 2299
Email: books@troubador.co.uk
Web: www.troubador.co.uk/matador
Twitter: @matadorbooks

ISBN 978 1803136 844

British Library Cataloguing in Publication Data.
A catalogue record for this book is available from the British Library.

Printed and bound in Great Britain by 4edge Limited
Typeset in 11pt Minion Pro by Troubador Publishing Ltd, Leicester, UK

Matador is an imprint of Troubador Publishing Ltd

In memory of my dear Granny
And her beloved brother, John

Per ardua ad astra
"Through adversity to the stars."
The motto of the RAF

CHAPTER 1

Everything started to unravel for Eliza the day she found the dead frog. Not that the frog itself had much to do with anything, but if she had to pinpoint a moment in time when she began to feel her ship was sinking. That was it.

'Do you think we should bury it?' Eliza asked her best friend.

'Definitely,' Anaya replied. 'Everyone deserves a burial, even frogs.'

'We should take it back to my house and bury it by the pond,' said Eliza.

'Perfect place,' said Anaya. 'I think he'd like that.'

It was a shared love of animals that first united Eliza and Anaya right at the very beginning. When they were tiny things with tidy hair and too-big school uniforms. Nearly seven years later and they'd hardly spent a school day apart.

Eliza took out her lunchbox and tipped the sandwich crusts and apple core into the empty crisp bag.

'We can put him in here,' she said.

Being the least squeamish of the two, Eliza scooped up the frog and laid it carefully in the lunchbox.

'Urgh!' came a voice from over her shoulder. 'I knew you were disgusting Eliza, but killing frogs and taking them home for your tea is just so weird.'

Why was it that Amy Cotter always turned up at exactly the wrong time?

Eliza's cheeks glowed furiously as she shoved the lid on her lunchbox and stood up.

'We didn't kill the frog,' said Anaya. 'Maybe it saw your sour face and just dropped dead.'

Amy started to say something but Anaya was a step ahead.

'Come on Elz,' she said, ignoring Amy and tucking her arm through Eliza's.

'You were brilliant,' Eliza said as they walked up the road together, leaving Amy pouting behind them.

'Have a go Elz,' said Anaya. 'She'd soon stop bothering you if you do.'

Eliza looked at her friend.

'Are you serious?' she said. 'Amy would eat me alive. I'm not like you. They'd better put us in the same class in September. I don't think I could walk into that massive high-school without you Anaya.'

Anaya looked at Eliza in a way that made her hair prickle with worry.

'What is it?' Eliza asked.

Anaya took a deep breath.

'I've been trying to tell you all week Elz. I just couldn't find the right time.'

'What?' Eliza demanded.

'You know that boarding school I told you about?'

'The one in Nottingham?' Eliza said, a terrible thought starting to poke at her. She shoved it aside. 'The one your mum made you have a look around but you decided not to go?'

'We couldn't afford it,' Anaya said. 'But...'

No Eliza thought. *No 'buts'. Stop there. You can't afford it so you're not going. You're coming to Highmoor Comp with me. Eliza and Anaya, just like it's always been.*

'But, we got a letter last week. They've offered me a ballet scholarship.'

'And you said no?'

'Elz, I had to say yes. It's an amazing opportunity. I get to study with some of the best ballet teachers of...'

'NO!' Eliza yelled. 'You can't!

Eliza's blood ran ice cold and boiling hot at the same time. Tears filled her eyes and she scrubbed them away angrily with her arm.

'Eliza, please don't be like this,' Anaya said.

If she'd stopped to think about it, Eliza would have known she wasn't being fair. But at that moment, somewhere near her heart, she felt an ache so strong that it pushed away everything except hurt and anger.

'Just go then,' she shouted. 'Go and do your thing in Nottingham.'

The tears overspilled and tumbled down Eliza's cheeks, dripping from her chin. Anaya reached her hand across the gap that had grown between them, and Eliza was about to take it when Amy flounced up to them. She pushed past Eliza making her drop the lunchbox onto the pavement where the lid popped off and the frog fell out.

'Eliza the El-loser,' she hissed.

Eliza looked at Amy's gloating face and then at Anaya's worried one. It was all too much. She scooped the frog back into the box, jammed on the lid and ran away from both girls. She ran with unstoppable tears, and only slowed when she reached her own front door.

* * *

Eliza stood on the doorstep for a moment, giving herself time to slow down her breathing and stop the tears.

Lazy summer rain began to drip, drip in that gentle way it does before the heavens open. The hot pavement gained a new dark spot with each drop that hit it. Eliza breathed in the smell of the thirsty world, getting its first drink for weeks. Instead of rushing inside, she tipped her head back, blinking each time a raindrop hit her. She shut her eyes and let them come. Slow at first, and then faster and faster. Big drops, pelting her face, her hair, her outstretched arms. Eliza wished they could wash away the rubbish day. Scrub out the memories of Amy. Make her forget what had happened with Anaya.

'Eliza,' Dad called through the window of his downstairs office. 'Get inside before you're soaked through.'

He was working from home then, Eliza thought. She imagined what it would be like to go inside and rush into his office. Climb onto his knee like she had when she was little and bury her face into his chest whilst he stroked her hair to make everything better. Or perhaps to find Mum inside, apron on, baking something nice for pudding. There with big arms to hug her and ready ears to listen to her problems.

But since Mum had gone back to work full time and Dad had got his promotion, neither of them ever had any time spare for her these days.

'Eliza,' Dad shouted. 'I told you to come inside.'

Eliza sighed. She unlocked the front door slowly and Boo came skidding round the corner, as pleased to see her as always. Boo, the Jack Russell, was almost as old as Eliza was. Granny P had got him as a puppy soon after Eliza had been born, and he'd come to live with them two years later when Granny P decided to move to Greece.

Eliza bent down and scratched Boo between the ears.

'Hi Boodle Boo,' she whispered into his wiry fur. 'Hope your day's been better than mine.' He waggled his funny, shaggy eyebrows at her and flipped over onto his back so she could give his tummy a good tickle.

'Come on Boo,' she said. 'I've got a frog to bury before Mum finds it and chucks it in the bin.'

The funeral seemed so important when Anaya had been coming home to do it with her. But now that she was on her own, it didn't feel quite the same.

'Everything alright, Eliza darling?' called her great-granny from the sitting room.

Eliza went in with Boo at her heels and kissed Ganny's wrinkled forehead before sitting down on the sofa next to her. Boo didn't wait to be asked before jumping up and settling himself across Eliza's knee like a blanket.

'Hi Ganny,' she said to her favourite person in the world.

'How was school?' Ganny asked. 'Did Mrs Sutton like your history project?'

'She gave me four house points,' Eliza said. 'You were

right. The carrot fudge and beetroot cake were much better than just another poster.'

'In my experience, teachers always like homework they can eat,' Ganny grinned.

Nobody else in Eliza's class had had help with their World War II project from someone who could actually remember it.

'Feeling glum?' Ganny asked. And Eliza realised she must look a mess, sitting there in her soaked school uniform, wet hair scraped back from a face crumpled from crying.

'A little,' she said.

'Care to share?'

'I found a dead frog,' Eliza said.

'Oh, now that is sad,' Ganny said.

'And I had a row with Anaya.'

'I see,' said Ganny. 'A rough day all round then.'

Eliza felt miserable as two tears spilled from her eyes without warning.

'A cuddle I think,' said Ganny. 'You're never too old for a cuddle to help with the glums.'

Ganny opened her arms and Eliza shuffled along the sofa until she was snuggled up next to her great-gran's warm, comfy body. Ever since she was little, Ganny was the person Eliza felt happiest with. It didn't matter how much the black clouds gathered and swamped her mind, Ganny was always there to calm her down and cheer her up.

'I brought the frog home with me,' Eliza said.

'Then we must have a funeral,' said Ganny. 'The rain is definitely easing up. As soon as it stops, we'll go out and bury him by the pond.'

'That's exactly where Anaya and I thought,' said Eliza, fresh tears beginning to form as she thought about the way she'd treated her friend.

'Shall we give her a ring?' Ganny said gently. 'Perhaps she'd like to join us?'

Eliza shook her head. 'Not today.'

'Alright,' said Ganny. 'But don't leave it too long to make up. The longer you leave it, the harder it gets.'

CHAPTER 2

The sun came out as Eliza dug a little hole in the wet ground at the edge of the pond. Ganny picked some rose petals and dropped them into the hole for Eliza to lay the frog onto. Boo stared at the frog and then at Eliza before trotting back, snaffling his way through the flowerbeds in the hope of finding something more exciting than a frog's funeral.

'Do you think he had a name?' Ganny asked.

Eliza thought about it. If she was a frog, being buried by strangers, she wouldn't like them to guess her name and bury her with the wrong one.

'No,' she said.

'Then perhaps we just remember him as Sir Froggy.'

Eliza nodded. She covered the frog with more rose petals and filled the hole with the little pile of earth she had dug out.

Ganny pointed at a large stone with her walking stick. 'See if you can push that over the mound,' she said. 'Just to make sure nothing decides to come along and dig poor old Sir Froggy back up again.'

When they had finished, Eliza took Ganny's arm and walked with her back inside.

'Tea, toast and Backgammon?' Ganny asked.

'Best idea,' said Eliza, smiling just a little at the soothing effect of Ganny's company.

* * *

Ganny's fingers, with knuckles that seemed far too large for them, pushed the last of her Backgammon pieces off the board.

'I think that's one win each,' she said. Her pale eyes sparkled, surrounded by wrinkles and crinkles from a life spent finding things to smile at. 'Line them up for the decider, Sweetpea, I'm feeling lucky!'

'Don't be too sure about that,' Eliza said, separating the pieces into two piles and passing the black ones over to Ganny.

'John would play Backgammon with me when I was your age,' Ganny said. 'Even though chess was really his game. He'd always find the time for a game of Backgammon because he knew how much I loved it.'

John was Ganny's older brother. He'd been in the RAF during World War II and died when he was just nineteen years old. On the little table next to the sofa where Ganny always sat, she'd put a big black and white photo of him. There was also a photo of her only daughter, Granny P, on the beach in Greece and another of Eliza with Mum and Dad. But the photo of John was by far the biggest and Eliza loved it.

'He looks like you,' she said, going over and picking up the heavily framed picture.

'Do you think so?'

Eliza looked at John and then back at Ganny, imagining what she would have been like as a teenager.

'I really do,' she said.

John had the same enormous smile as Ganny. He looked like the sort of person who would be just as brilliant at playing funny tricks on people as he was at helping them out whenever he could. Friendly, playful eyes beamed at the camera from under the RAF cap he proudly wore. The same cap that now sat under a blue and white china plaque of Mary and Jesus in Ganny's room.

'I wish I had a brother,' Eliza said.

'You can share John with me,' said Ganny.

She focussed on the chair opposite.

'What do you think, John?' she asked the empty space, waiting for a moment before turning back to Eliza.

'He says he'd like that very much.'

Eliza grinned. She was used to seeing Ganny talk to her dead brother. It was something she'd done ever since she'd recovered from the stroke that had made it unsafe for her to stay in her own home. The stroke that had brought her to live with them, two years earlier.

'What did you talk about today?' Eliza asked.

'We talked about the tennis club we used to go to every weekend. We both loved to play, although I was by far the better player.'

Ganny lifted one eyebrow up as she said this and smiled at the empty chair. There was a pause as though she was listening.

'You may choose to remember in your way, but I will choose to remember in mine. And as I have told you a thousand times, dearest brother, I am always right!'

Eliza watched her great grandmother as she chatted to the empty chair for a little while longer. Her eyes bright and her cheeks rosy as she giggled at jokes and memories from her childhood. If Mum and Dad had been there, they'd have tried to stop her. Told her that John wasn't there. But what did it really matter? Ganny was always so happy when she thought she was talking to John.

'You must think I'm an old fool,' said Ganny.

'I don't,' Eliza said, honestly.

'Just between you and me, I think your parents might.'

'Who cares?' said Eliza, suddenly feeling angry. 'They're hardly ever here anyway. And when they are, they're either working or just too tired to do anything.'

'Don't be too harsh with them, Sweetpea,' said Ganny. 'They do love you very much. I don't have to have perfect eyesight to see that.'

Eliza sighed. 'Maybe,' she said, snuggling back in for an extra hug. 'But I'm still glad I've got you.'

＊ ＊ ＊

On her way up to bed that night, Eliza noticed the lamp in the empty office was on so she went in to switch it off. As she leant over the desk, something caught her eye. Propped up at the back of the desk was a pile of brochures. The one at the front had a picture of a lady with a silver hair bun, laughing whilst she pushed the wheelchair of a bald man, wrapped in a brightly knitted blanket.

FROBISHER'S CARE HOME, it said underneath.

Eliza picked the pile up and looked through. There were five of them altogether, each for a different care home and each with pictures of old people smiling as though being stuck in a care home was the best thing ever. Eliza scowled at the brochures with a feeling in her stomach like she'd just swallowed a bag of worms.

She put them back, switched off the lamp and went upstairs. By the time she'd got her pyjamas on and burrowed down with Alfie Bear under her duvet, the worms had turned into enormous eels, all squirming and twisting inside her.

Eliza hugged Alfie Bear tight and tried hard not to let the dark clouds in. But the day had been a tough one. Tougher than most.

And now this. The thought of Ganny not being in the house any more was too much for Eliza. She closed her eyes and tried to stop the eels squirming in her stomach by hugging herself tightly and rocking slightly from side to side. But it didn't work. She felt lost and lonely and totally helpless. If only there was a way to stop these things from happening. A way of keeping the people she loved close to her, but it was something she had absolutely no control over. Her fists clenched with the hopelessness of it all and her entire body tensed as every muscle tightened. Her teeth and jaws clamped together and her eyes ached, firing darts of light and colour across her vision from the pressure of being squeezed shut.

The energy and pain built until Eliza couldn't keep it in any longer. She took her tightly wound frustration out on her pillow, punching and hitting as she cried until finally her breathing slowed and her face relaxed.

She knew her parents' game. But if they were planning on taking Ganny away and packing her off to one of those stuffy old homes, then she certainly wasn't going to make it easy for them.

CHAPTER 3

The next morning, Eliza lay in bed listening as first Mum and then Dad got up. Saturdays always meant the same thing. Dad trying to ease his *work stress* with a mega session at the gym whilst Mum met up with her friends for a *catch up walk and coffee.*

Eliza pretended she was still sleeping when they came in to say goodbye. But, as soon as the door banged shut for the second time, she got out of bed and went to make Ganny a cup of tea. Ganny was sitting up in bed watching kids' cartoons and chuckling to herself.

'It's not as good as Tom and Jerry,' she said when Eliza walked in. 'But I still think cartoons are the best thing for a Saturday morning.'

'I've got you a cup of tea,' said Eliza. 'Earl Grey with no milk.'

'Thank you, Sweetpea,' said Ganny, taking the cup. 'There's room for a little one if you want to squidge in and have some toon time with me.'

As Eliza swung her legs up onto the bed, Ganny put her hand on Eliza's knee.

'What's the matter, Poppet?'

'Nothing,' said Eliza.

'I know that beautiful face of yours better than I know my own and I can see you've been crying again. Have you spoken to Mum and Dad about your worries?'

Eliza shook her head roughly.

'What's the point?' she said. 'They don't care about me. Nobody does except you and Boo.'

Ganny put her arm around Eliza and pulled her into a hug.

'They might surprise you, you know,' she said.

Eliza didn't say that they'd already surprised her enough with the bundle of brochures she'd found.

'Did you ever hear from John when he was in the RAF?' Eliza said, expertly changing the subject.

'He did write now and again,' said Ganny. 'Mainly when he was still based at Hartwell, not far from Reading. When he was sent to Malta, getting letters home was much trickier and they came with big parts blacked out so we couldn't always tell what he was saying.'

Eliza knew from her topic work at school that all letters sent home were censored to make sure nobody could pass on sensitive information, either by mistake or on purpose.

'How long was he out in Malta?' Eliza asked.

'Almost a year and a half. He was sent over in the summer of 1941. Went out with the rest of his squadron to help clear the skies over Malta. That poor island had been having a bit of a bashing from the Italian planes, and things only got worse when Hitler's Luftwaffe got involved. John ended up in the thick of it and watched the island under siege until September of 1942.'

'Where was he sent after that?' Eliza asked.

Ganny's face crumpled.

'There wasn't an *after that*,' she said. 'Not for John anyway. His plane was lost. All six of the crewmen on it too. Somewhere over the Mediterranean Sea.'

'Sorry,' said Eliza. She knew he'd died in the war of course, but it made her very wobbly to think of the smiling man in the black and white photo disappearing over the sea, leaving behind a family who didn't know exactly what had happened to him.'

'Poor John can't help,' Ganny said. 'I only asked him once what happened. But he couldn't remember. Either that or he didn't want to.'

Ganny's eyes swam as she talked about her brother. Eighty years had passed but the memory of his death was clearly something that had never gone away. It was the first time that Ganny had mentioned talking to John as a ghost that made Eliza feel uncomfortable. Up until then it had been a bit of fun. She knew it wasn't real and she thought Ganny did too, deep down. But there was something different about it this time, maybe because of the care home brochures.

Neither Eliza nor Ganny spoke for a minute or two, each lost in their own thoughts.

'Oh, good heavens!' Ganny broke the silence with a loud explosion of laughter. 'Would you look at that.'

She pointed at the television and Eliza smiled too as a cartoon dog tried again and again to fit an enormous stick through a very small gap.

'Do you know what would make this even funnier?'

Ganny said. 'If he went and fetched his tool kit and cut out a perfect, stick-sized slot for it to go through.'

Ganny's temporary black cloud had lifted quickly and her sparkling, bright eyes were back.

You see, Eliza thought, *bright as a button and sharp as a pin.*

People kept saying it, and people were right. Eliza didn't know anyone as bright or as sharp as Ganny. And if someone was as bright as a button and as sharp as a pin, then surely there was no good reason at all to ship them off to a home for old folk. Although maybe it wouldn't hurt to lay off the ghost talk for a little while.

* * *

That afternoon, Dad was watching old films on his own to give his brain a rest from the busy week. Mum had some work she just needed to rush through, so she borrowed Dad's office and shut the door behind her. Usually, Eliza would have called Anaya and met up in the park or over at her house. There was a huge part of her that desperately wanted to see her best friend. She knew she'd been unfair to Anaya when she found out about the boarding school and she wanted to say sorry. But it wouldn't change the horridness of the fact she was still going to be leaving. In September, Eliza would have to walk into that enormous new school on her own.

In the end it was a mixture of embarrassment and anger that stopped Eliza from calling. Instead, she laid on her bed reading for a while and then played Backgammon with Ganny.

They were only halfway through a game though, when Ganny looked at the empty chair across from her and smiled at it as if John was sitting there. For the first time, Eliza didn't see the good in this tiny action that made Ganny so happy. This time all she saw was a crazy old woman who either kept on pretending she was talking to her long dead brother or worse, actually believed that she was. Eliza tried to ignore the bad feeling that started to slip inside her.

'Your turn Ganny,' she said.

Ganny rolled the dice.

'A two and a four,' she said, looking at her pieces on the board. 'I think I'll take you with this one, and then use the four to move either this, or this.'

She looked at the chair again.

'Which one, hmm? This or this?'

Something inside Eliza snapped. She could almost feel it. The weight of worry that had piled up so high, now topped with the thought of losing first Anaya and now Ganny. Why did Ganny have to do this? She was just giving them more reasons to send her off to the old folks' home.

'He's not there,' she snapped. 'Look, just look won't you?'

'Sweetpea?' Ganny said.

'I'm sorry,' Eliza sobbed. 'But he's not. And you're just making it worse.'

She pushed the Backgammon board away from her, making the pieces slide. Then she ran up to her room, two stairs at a time, until she was on her bed. Face first in the pillows, hands raking through her hair, trying to get rid of all the dark thoughts that crowded her mind.

'Eliza!' Mum's voice boomed from downstairs. 'Whatever's going on? I'm trying to work and it's a really difficult project so I could do without all the stomping.'

Eliza clamped her hands over her ears to block Mum out.

After a little while, there was a gentle tapping on Eliza's door.

'Sweetpea?' Ganny called softly through the tiny gap she'd pushed open. 'Can I come in?'

Eliza didn't say anything so Ganny came over and sat on the edge of the bed.

'I think we could do with a bit of a chat, don't you?' Ganny said.

Eliza rolled over so she could see Ganny properly.

'I'm really sorry I shouted at you,' she said.

'Oh, don't worry about that,' Ganny smiled. 'I'm certainly not. No, I'm far more worried about you, my darling. You have a lot on your mind and I'm sorry if I make things worse by talking to John.'

'You really think he's here, don't you?' Eliza sniffed, searching Ganny's face.

'Let me tell you a little something I've learned about ghosts,' said Ganny. 'It seems most of the time, they just keep away. But now and again, only when we really need them and only when we are open to the idea of seeing them, they pay us a visit.'

Eliza reached across the bed and took hold of Ganny's hand. It may have been almost one hundred years old, but the hand could still manage a good firm squeeze and it still had the power to make Eliza feel that little bit better.

'But you never used to speak to him before,' Eliza said.

'I was far too busy to notice that I could,' Ganny said. 'And John was patient. He waited until I really needed his company, and then he came.'

'After your stroke?'

'Yes, I suppose it was. Not straight away, not with all those physiotherapists and doctors and nurses with me all the time. Not to mention all my old friends who kept popping by for a chat.'

'So, when then?' Eliza asked.

'When things started to go quiet,' Ganny said, gently. 'When I moved here and left all my friends behind me.'

'But I'm here!' said Eliza.

'You are indeed, my darling. And you bring me more joy than anything else. But there are still an awful lot of lonely hours to fill, sitting here watching the garden change through the seasons. And John fills it.'

Eliza stared at the swirly pattern on her duvet cover and began tracing the lines with her fingers. She hadn't ever really stopped to think about what it had been like for Ganny to move away from her home. She'd always just assumed that she loved living with them as much as Eliza loved having her.

'I'm sorry you miss your friends,' she said, quietly.

'But I have you, my darling, darling girl. And I have John. Both of you bring me more comfort and happiness than you will ever know.'

Eliza stopped herself from pointing out that only one of them was real. It shouldn't matter. If pretending she could talk to her brother made Ganny happy then why shouldn't she? But the terrible thought of the care home brochures refused to leave Eliza alone. She dropped her head and sighed deeply.

'I have something for you,' Ganny said, pulling a book out of the pocket of her baggy cardigan.

Eliza took it and turned it over. It was an old-fashioned black notebook with a feathered pattern down the spine and gold paint sprayed down the edges of the pages. The front cover had a small white label stuck on it and Ganny had written JOHN in curly capital letters.

'It was very difficult to get word back to us when he was stationed in Malta with the RAF,' Ganny said. 'But since he's come back to visit, he's been filling me with his memories and I in turn have been filling this book with them.'

Eliza opened the first page.

England – January 1941, it read.

'It's hard to read in some places,' Ganny went on. 'But I think you're old enough now. And I shall love to have someone else to talk about it with. Maybe it will help him become more real to you too, who knows? Will you read it?'

'Well...' stammered Eliza.

Ganny's curly writing wasn't the easiest of things to read, and Eliza wasn't all that sure she wanted to encourage the ghost talking. It might speed up the process of pushing Ganny into the old people's home.

'I would hate for his story to be forgotten when it's my time to leave this life,' Ganny said. Tears sparkled in her eyes and Eliza found her own eyes joining in.

'I'll read it,' she promised.

Ganny squeezed her hand once more before leaving the book on the bed and closing the door gently on her way out.

Eliza stared at the first page. She didn't really want to, but she'd made a promise and she'd seen what that promise meant to Ganny. So, she pulled Alfie Bear into a hug and settled down to read.

CHAPTER 4

ENGLAND – JANUARY 1941

The day I decided to volunteer for the RAF was one of the wettest I think I'd ever seen. I was still just seventeen, not yet old enough to enrol but I knew they were desperate for fit young men, and as many of us as possible, so I thought I'd try my luck.

Mother was furious with me. But not as furious as she was with my father who agreed to help me falsify my papers. I thought she was going to take her rolling pin and give him what for. I remember Father telling her that if she didn't calm down, the army would be sure to try and recruit her too. Never was there a more fearsome weapon than Mother when she was angry!

'He's almost eighteen,' Father said. 'The same age I was when I went to fight in the trenches of France. And, I might add, when you first donned your nurse's uniform and went out to the army hospital in Belgium.'

'Yes,' Mother said. 'And we both saw first-hand just what war did to our men. What it did to you.'

She poked at his gammy leg, the one with shrapnel still embedded in it.

'We did,' Father said, rather grim-faced. 'And we would both do it again if we were able. This war affects every one of us and if John is willing to play his part then we must send him off with our love and all the luck we can give him.'

I think that was when Mother saw my going as inevitable. If not straight away, then when I turned eighteen a few months later and the choice was no longer mine. She hugged me so tightly I wondered if she might be trying to crack my ribs to give me a reason to stay behind.

When I finally managed to untangle myself from Mother's apron, I noticed my little sister, Elizabeth, standing with her hands behind her back in that way she always did when she was nervous or worried.

'Come here Liffy,' I said, holding my arms out. For a moment I thought she might refuse. As a small child, Liffy had always been so stubborn and as a teenager she was doubly so. But my charms were too much and she hugged me tight.

'How long have we got you for,' she asked.

'I'm not sure,' I said. 'I'm going to London tomorrow to sit the entrance exam and then who knows? It might not be all that long, so we'd better make the most of it. Tea, toast and Backgammon?'

* * *

I don't mind admitting that once Father had agreed to my signing up and it became a real prospect, I felt at once excited and terrified. I wasn't naive. I knew that flying with the RAF was dangerous and that many, many pilots had already lost their lives and countless others would follow in their suit. But I was also someone who had always been fascinated by aeroplanes and now I was getting the chance to learn to fly. Besides, I think I felt invincible in those days, certain that I would see the end of the war and return home a hero.

There was one person I wanted to share my adventure with more than anyone. Bill Chandler, the very best of men and my truest friend since we'd been in short trousers. We would tear around the streets with our arms open wide, dive bombing each other as we made the sounds of our aeroplane engines. Of course, I assumed that, when he heard I was volunteering for the RAF, he was bound to do the same and we would naturally join the same squadron. Once the rain finally stopped and I'd been beaten by Liffy at Backgammon more times than is reasonable, I ran round to Bill's house and banged on the door.

'Oh, it's you John,' said Bill's father as he opened the door. I noticed he looked very pale and a little unwell, but I didn't pay it much attention. 'You'd better come in. Bill's in the kitchen with Mrs Chandler.'

I walked in and found Bill with his arm around his mother. Her face was ever so red and blotchy and I could tell at once that she'd been crying.

'Oh John,' Mrs Chandler sighed. 'Take this child of mine away and try and talk some sense into him. He seems to be intent on killing himself in the name of this blasted war.'

'Mother,' said Bill, going a little red around the cheeks.

I felt dreadfully sorry for Mr and Mrs Chandler. But I also felt a little spark of excitement. It sounded as though

Bill was a step ahead. Perhaps I wouldn't have to persuade him to join the RAF with me. He may have already decided to do just that himself.

'I'll get my coat,' Bill said and we were soon out of the door and walking towards the old park with our collars up and caps pulled down to protect us from the still damp, cold air.

'Do I take it you're signing up?' I asked.

'I felt it was my duty to,' Bill said. 'And anyway, I turn eighteen next week so it really wouldn't be all that long before I have no choice about it.'

'I had the same thought,' I said. 'I spoke to Mother and Father about it today.'

'Well, I never,' Bill chuckled. 'And how have your parents taken it?'

'Much the same as yours by the look of it. Liffy looked pretty miserable I have to admit. But she's fifteen, she'll soon be so busy with other young men who capture her attention that she won't have time to waste thinking about me.'

'It'll be a lucky chap who wins her heart,' Bill said.

'But it won't be you I'm afraid Bill,' I chuckled.

'Damn shame,' Bill grinned back.

'Gosh, what a lot has changed since we first zoomed around this very park in our make-believe planes,' I said, nudging Bill in the ribs.

'Our poor mothers had no chance of quietening us,' said Bill.

'And now we'll be off learning to fly the real things. I think our young selves would be very proud, don't you?' I said. 'I'm so terribly glad we're in this together. I don't think I'd feel nearly so brave if I was going completely on my own.

I'm planning on going to Euston House tomorrow to sign up and sit the exam. We can go together if you think your parents will let you. If not, then I can wait a week and we can go when you're officially old enough to...'

It was then that I realised Bill's face had dropped.

'What is it?' I asked.

'I'm not signing up to the RAF,' Bill said.

'What on earth do you mean?' I said. 'You just told me...'

'I told you I'd signed up,' Bill replied. 'But zooming around a field as boys is one thing. I share your passion for aeroplanes from an engineering point of view. But I'm not cut out for life as a pilot. I don't think I'd survive my first take off.'

'But it was always going to be the RAF for us,' I spluttered in shock. 'You can't possibly want an army life can you? Surely not after what both our fathers went through in the trenches.'

'Actually, I've not signed up for the army either,' said Bill. 'I'm going to be a naval cadet. Life on the ocean blue and all that. I've always loved radios, you know that. I'm pretty sharp with Morse Code already. Enough to have been accepted into the naval training programme as a telegraphist.'

'Hang on,' I said. 'You've already signed up? In secret?'

John looked a little abashed.

'I knew my parents would try to stop me so I just bit the bullet and went for it. They could see I was underage from my papers but just by a week so they ignored it. Besides I'll most probably have turned eighteen by the time I'm called.'

'I don't believe you,' I said. And, to my eternal shame, I felt overcome with rage. 'How could you make such a terrible decision?'

'John!'

'No,' I said. 'I wish you well in your naval life, Bill. But right now I'm going home.'

I didn't even shake his hand. I just turned around and left Bill in the park. That was the last I saw of Bill Chandler. Two days later I went to London on my own and sat the exam and had my medical checks. Something about seeing the city and all the young men in uniform heading off to fight made me instantly regret my behaviour towards Bill. As soon as I got back, I went round to apologise but it was already too late. His number had been called and he'd left for Plymouth and his new life with the navy. The regret I felt at my behaviour towards my dear friend Bill was something that would never leave me.

The following day I received word that I'd passed my exams with flying colours but that I wasn't going to be a pilot.

'The radios Bill and I built and the fact that he made me learn Morse Code with him make me perfect to join as a trainee wireless operator,' I told my family.

'That'll make Bill laugh,' said Liffy when she heard the news. 'I remember him nagging you like a school mistress to learn Morse Code so you could play his games with him. Funny that you are now putting it to good use!'

I wished I could tell Bill but I had no idea when he'd next be granted leave to visit home or if I'd still be there when he did.

* * *

Shortly after, I received the news that my family had been dreading. I was given my orders and sent to Warrington to be kitted out before heading to Blackpool to begin my training.

It was awful saying goodbye to my family. Trying to keep my top lip from wobbling as I kissed my mother and shook my father's hand. But it was Liffy who made it even harder. Liffy, with her straight back and determination to be brave. The hug she gave that told me just how much she would miss me. How much we'd miss each other.

'I made this for you,' she said. 'Out of scraps.'

She passed me a tiny rabbit made from soft brown velvet with a dress the same fabric as the one Liffy herself was wearing.

'She's called Susan Rabbit and she's incredibly lucky,' said Liffy. 'You must promise to keep her in your pocket the whole time. Every day you must kiss her nose for good luck until the day she brings you safely back home again.'

I couldn't find any words at that point. I kissed Liffy one last time and tucked Susan Rabbit into my pocket.

And that was it, I was off to Warrington then Blackpool, Wiltshire and finally RAF Hartwell in Berkshire where I would learn how to be a wireless operator and gunner. And even more terrifyingly, I'd learn pretty quickly how to be an adult.

CHAPTER 5

Eliza put the book down on her bedside table. It felt like someone else's story and yet some of the characters were so familiar. She knew she'd been named after her great-grandmother but she'd always just called her Ganny. To see her name on the page, Liffy – short for Elizabeth, just as Eliza was. And to think of her as a fifteen-year-old girl. How awful it must have been for her to say goodbye to her big brother, not knowing if she'd ever see him again.

The whole weekend, Eliza thought about Anaya. She didn't want to have the same regrets as John had when Bill left. But every time she reached for the phone, something stopped her. By Monday morning, things felt worse than ever. She left home so late that Anaya had gone without her. When she got to school, she went into the classroom just as Mrs Sutton was finishing the register.

'Nice to have you with us, Eliza,' said Mrs Sutton over the top of her reading glasses. 'Kindly take this back to the office as you're on your feet.'

She held out the register and Eliza's cheeks burned at the attention as she took it. She dropped it in the register box outside the office and went back to class, sitting in the empty seat closest to the door so that she didn't have to cross the classroom to get to her usual space next to Anaya.

'Right then, Year 6,' said Mrs Sutton. 'As you are well aware, tomorrow marks your last ever day of Colderstone Primary.'

The louder kids in the class started whooping, and the quieter ones punched the air or grinned. Some of the girls hugged each other and a couple dabbed at their faces as though trying not to cry at the thought.

Eliza stared at the table in front of her.

'Yes, yes. Settle down, settle down.'

If she'd been sitting next to Anaya, they'd be giggling at the way Mrs Sutton said things twice. Eliza glanced over at her friend, hoping that she might catch her eye and break the horridness between them. But Anaya wasn't sitting on her own. Amy was sitting in Eliza's usual seat.

Eliza looked away quickly and stared down at the table again.

'I thought it might be nice for us to make a book of messages and memories for you all to take away. Greta and Asha, could you hand these bits of paper around please. I want you all to write something nice to your classmates. Think of a way you wish to be remembered. Make them as bright and colourful as you like and then I'll scan them into the computer and print out enough for all of you. This afternoon we can sew the pages together so you all have your own book to take home.'

It felt strange and horrible, sitting on the wrong side of

the room. Instead of sharing colouring pencils and squishy rubbers with Anaya, she had to put up with Nial and Davide, who found it funny to try and draw on her work and flick her with bits of scabby old rubber they'd pulled apart.

Eliza looked at the piece of paper in front of her wondering what on earth she was supposed to write to a bunch of people who had spent the past seven years ignoring her. She stole a look at Anaya and saw Amy, whispering something into her ear. Something that made Anaya giggle. Amy noticed Eliza watching and smirked.

Eliza felt hot all of a sudden. They *must* have been talking about her. And by the way Anaya had giggled, she obviously agreed with whatever Amy had been saying.

The heat spilled from her face and ran down her entire body. Her eyes started to swim and breathing was suddenly a lot trickier than it should have been.

'Eliza?' said a voice through her pounding head. 'Eliza? Are you alright?'

Eliza looked up and saw the shape of Mrs Sutton in front of her table.

'I think we'd better get you to the sick room.'

Why was her voice so muffled? And why were the lights suddenly so bright?

Eliza closed her eyes and blocked everything out whilst she counted her breaths in and out.

'Someone get Mrs Rogers,' Mrs Sutton said and Eliza felt an arm rest across her shoulders.

As quickly as the strangeness had come on, it started to leave again. By the time kind Mrs Rogers arrived and ushered Eliza out of the classroom and down to the sick room, she was already feeling much better. Well, her body was anyway.

'I've called your Mum and Dad,' said Mrs Mitchener from the office. 'No answer from either of them but I've left a message with your great-gran so hopefully someone will come and get you very soon.'

'Thanks,' Eliza managed to say, not sharing Mrs Mitchener's hope.

'Lie down here,' said Mrs Rogers. 'I'll go and fetch the cards I was just sticking together for Mr Reeves and then I can keep you company until you get collected.'

It only took an hour for Dad to come. Luckily, he'd been working from home and had managed to pop out to fetch her, in between calls.

'How are you feeling now?' he asked in the car on the way home.

'Bit better,' Eliza said.

'You do look a bit peaky.'

He leant over and put his hand on her forehead and then chuckled.

'I don't know why I did that,' he said. 'I'm not really sure what counts as just warm, what counts as *too* warm and what counts as *fetch the doctor immediately* warm!'

Eliza smiled back.

'Thanks for coming to get me,' she said.

'Of course I came,' said Dad. 'Sorry not to get to you earlier. I was on a call and...'

'I know,' said Eliza. 'It's fine.'

When she got home, Eliza went straight upstairs and put her pyjamas on. Then she took a blanket from her bed and went down to snuggle up on the sofa with Ganny and Boo.

Ganny held her hand and Boo curled into a tight ball on her lap.

'Did you have a chance to talk to Anaya today, before you were sent home?' Ganny asked.

'She was sitting with someone else,' Eliza said. 'Someone who isn't actually very nice to people. I don't think today was the day to make up after all.'

Ganny nodded.

'Which princess will it be today?' she asked.

'What?'

'Poorly days can only be accompanied by one thing,' Ganny announced. 'Walt Disney.'

Eliza smiled and they decided, between them, to start at the beginning with Snow White.

Dad came in with two bowls of tomato soup at lunch time.

'How's the patient?' he asked.

'Better thanks,' said Eliza.

'Only two bowls?' Ganny asked. 'Do you not eat lunch these days, Matthew?'

'I've got a call in five minutes so I'll take mine in the office.'

Eliza wondered if this was what it was like every day for Ganny. When she had to go to school, was Ganny left on her own in front of the television all day? Still, it would be the summer holidays tomorrow and then Eliza would be there to spend every day with her.

'What was it like in the war?' Eliza asked as they slurped their soup. 'For you at home after John left I mean.'

'You've started to read the journal? Ganny asked.

'Yes,' said Eliza. 'I'm not very fast but I've got up as far as John leaving home.'

'Well, my writing is probably a bit shakier and more difficult to read than it used to be.'

'I think it's beautiful writing,' said Eliza. 'But maybe just a bit tricky to read quickly.'

'That's very kind,' said Ganny. 'What was the war like? It was horrid and wonderful at the same time, if that doesn't sound too strange. We worried about John and all our other brave souls out on the front line. But there was a wonderful spirit of togetherness as the whole country pulled as one. We rallied around and looked after each other in those days. We grew potatoes and carrots in our garden and swapped them with next door's cabbages and beetroot. It was the same with chickens. Lots of people in our street kept chickens for the eggs, but when it came to killing them for the meat, we just couldn't bring ourselves to do our own. We would swap them with our neighbours so we never ate the ones we'd reared ourselves.'

'I don't think I'd have liked killing anyone's chickens,' Eliza said.

'Father always did it for us. And I can tell you now, if you were hungry enough you'd eat whatever was put on the table. Rationing was tough but we found ways to make things stretch. We were some of the luckier ones, living away from the big cities.'

'In the journal it says that your mum was a nurse and your dad got hurt in the war,' said Eliza.

'Ah yes,' said Ganny. 'That was during The First World War, before I was born. The war to end all wars they called it. My father found it very hard when it happened all over again. He didn't often talk about it, but I know he felt the losses of his friends very deeply. When we were little, he said they died so our country would never have to live through such horror again.'

'And then Hitler happened.'

'Yes darling, and then Hitler happened.'

'Did your dad want to fight again, if his leg hadn't been injured?'

Ganny sighed deeply. 'I don't think he could have taken it, although many did of course. But he threw himself into the voluntary Home Guard. Every day he prepared for the event of a German invasion. And he taught me too. I made sandbags with him and learnt what to do in the event of a fire. He showed me the art of camouflage and made sure I knew how to drive a car by the time I was sixteen. In those days we didn't need a licence to drive.'

'What about your mum?' Eliza asked. 'What was she doing while you were learning to drive cars and put out fires?'

'Ah now, she was a member of the Women's Institute.'

'Mrs Sutton told us about them, the WI,' said Eliza. 'They made lots of jams and cakes.'

'That's right,' said Ganny. 'Well jams and pickles definitely. It was a great way of saving all the fruit so that we had things to eat all year round. Cakes though, now they were a bit of a luxury so we didn't have too many of those. And when we did, they weren't anything like the ones we have now.'

Eliza thought about the war time recipes she and Ganny had looked at when they made the carrot fudge.

'Parsnip and beetroot cakes you mean?' she said. 'Yeaurgh!'

'There was no choice,' said Ganny. 'Sugar, flour and butter were rationed. We couldn't waste what we had making cakes. And when there's no other choice, it's surprising how tasty root vegetables can be. We wouldn't leave a scrap, every slice would be eaten, sometimes toasted and dunked in tea when it had gone a bit too stale or hard for the teeth.'

Eliza pictured Ganny eating stale parsnip cake and thought that if anyone could find a way to enjoy it, it would be Ganny. She pulled her feet up onto the sofa and snuggled in further.

'Tell me more about what it was like,' she said.

'It was my mother and the WI who taught me to sew and knit. We made hundreds of pairs of socks and blankets to send out to the boys in the trenches. My father could remember how utterly dismal it was to sit in the bottom of a trench with wet socks and freezing toes, so we used some of our fabric rationing coupons to buy lovely thick wool and we made sock after sock after sock.'

Before Ganny could talk more about the Home Guard or the WI, there was a knock on the door.

'Let me get that,' said Ganny.

She stood up and Eliza passed her her sticks. Boo jumped down to go and see who it was too. A moment later, Ganny came back.

'It's Anaya,' she said. 'She wonders if you're feeling well enough for a chat?'

Eliza almost said yes. But then she remembered the giggle and the nasty look from Amy. Her face flushed again.

'I'm in my pyjamas,' she said. 'And I don't think I'm up for seeing anyone just now.'

Ganny raised her eyebrows ever so slightly and then went back to the door to tell Anaya that Eliza wasn't well enough for visitors.

'I won't ask,' said Ganny when she returned to the sofa. 'But tell if you wish.'

'Do you mind if I don't?' said Eliza. 'I just want to forget it.'

'Maybe tomorrow will be a better day for talking to Anaya,' said Ganny.

Eliza nodded.

'But darling, don't leave it too late.'

* * *

Eliza woke up on her last ever day at primary school feeling sick with nerves. She put on her uniform and sat at the breakfast table staring at the bowl of cornflakes in front of her. The thought of stepping back into the classroom again made her head swim. Amy and Anaya would probably be sitting together, giggling and making fun of her. She didn't want to be alone, watching all the other kids in the class hugging each other and promising to keep in touch and stay friends.

'Eat up Eliza,' said Mum. 'I can drop you off today if you like. I can't believe it's your last day at Colderstone Primary.'

She kissed Eliza on the top of her head. 'It feels like just a couple of years ago that Daddy and I took you in for your first ever day. You were such a sweet little thing. All big eyes and such a serious face. Socks pulled up and hair in a little red ribbon. You clung onto my hand so tightly and you didn't want to let Alfie Bear go. I had to promise to look after him and keep him with me all day so that he wouldn't miss you too much, do you remember?'

Eliza nodded.

'I didn't know what to do with myself that day,' said Mum. 'I worried about you every single minute and was in the playground half an hour early to pick you up. I was the first one there.'

She lent her chin gently on Eliza's head and scooped her hair up into a ponytail, tickling the top of her neck. Eliza wished she could tell Mum how much she'd loved it when she was around to worry about her. And how much she missed the time when Mum was there in the playground waiting for her to come out of school at the end of each day. But she decided it would only cause problems so she kept quiet.

'I didn't need to worry though,' said Mum. 'Because when you came out, it was hand in hand with Anaya and you both had enormous smiles on your faces.'

Eliza hadn't the energy to reply. She sat there staring at the soggy cereal.

'You need to eat something,' said Mum.

'I'm not hungry,' said Eliza.

'Look at me,' said Mum.

Eliza turned around to face her.

'You do look peaky. Will you be alright to go to school? I'd hate for you to miss your last day but I don't want to send you in if you're not well.'

Without realising it, Mum had just handed Eliza the very thing she needed. The perfect excuse to skip school and dodge everything that she wanted to avoid. And a day to read more of Uncle John's journal.

CHAPTER 6

THE MEDiTERRANEAN SEA - JULY 1941

Training with the RAF had been hard work. I felt a great sense of patriotism and pride every time I put on my uniform and took another step to readying myself to fight for my country. The days were long and I missed my family dreadfully. Leave was brief but precious, although it was to my great sadness and regret that Bill wasn't there when I went home.

I spent two months in Blackpool doing basic training and getting quicker at translating and using Morse Code. I enjoyed it there because, although it was freezing cold, we did our drills on the Promenade along the seafront. Then I was moved to Yatesbury in Wiltshire for further training at the technical school there.

In May, I was sent to RAF Hartwell to finish my air crew training. It was there that I met Jellicoe Hyde, an amazing navigator from Jamaica who arrived at Hartwell on the same day as I did. Our bunks were next to each other and we hit it off straight away.

'Happy Birthday old man,' said Jellicoe one morning, pulling me from my sleep. He nodded at the cards from home that I'd opened the previous day and set by my bunk.

Eighteen at last. Officially old enough to fight in the war just weeks before our call came at the end of July.

Our squadron, Squadron 38 was sent by aircraft carrier to Malta in the Mediterranean Sea. Hundreds of miles from home. In fact, miles from any British base. The closest land by far was Italy to the north, and the coast of Africa to the south, held by Hitler's forces. Enemies all around, and boy was that clear when we arrived.

'Come on John,' said Jellicoe as we kitted up on the aircraft carrier that had been our floating home since we left England's shores to sail to the Mediterranean. 'Did you take this long to get ready to leave the house or did your Mama still do everything for you?' he joked.

'My mother always taught me that it's important to dress with care no matter what the occasion,' I replied. 'Something your mother obviously forgot to mention to you.'

Jellicoe gave a throaty laugh.

'You got me there,' he said. 'But you'd better move or we'll have Sheepy on our case.'

Flight Lieutenant Elmer Mutton, or Sheepy as we all affectionately called him, was our pilot and senior. He was already at the Wellington Bomber on the deck of the ship when we arrived.

'Good to see you chaps,' he said. 'Warm, isn't it?'

The rich, blue sky above was cloudless and the sea below was calm and inviting.

'Shame we can't go for a dip,' I said.

'I could help you with that,' Jellicoe said. 'Throw you overboard if that's what you want.'

'Come on you pair of clowns,' said Sheepy. 'The three gunners are already aboard and it would be nice if the navigator and radio operator could join us.'

'After you,' Jellicoe said, holding his arm out to me.

'Always the gentleman,' I joked as I climbed into the Wellington Bomber that would take me off the aircraft carrier and make the final leg of the journey to the island of Malta. 'Here we go,' I called down to Jellicoe but he couldn't hear over the roar of the engines.'

I kissed the nose of little Susan Rabbit and tucked her safely into my pocket. My heart was thumping and my head felt clammy and uncomfortable under my flying helmet. I flexed my fingers and tried to shake the enormous bundle of nerves that was coursing through me. Sheepy switched on the engine and I made final radio checks in preparation for take-off. The plane in front of us sped off down the runway and was soon in the sky, banking to the left and away she went.

'Chocks away,' shouted a chap who had cleared the blocks from our Wellington's wheels.

'This is it!' Sheepy shouted. 'Time to make it count boys.'

We'd taken off many times before. But never from an aircraft carrier in the middle of an ocean. The familiar radio controls felt good in my hands and I relaxed just a little as we cleared the deck and sped off over the blueness of the sea. I focussed on the messages coming in and clicked back my replies to base. The sky in front of us was dotted with other planes, all on our way to Malta. Men I hadn't known when the year began just a few short months ago. But men who were now my firm friends and who I trusted with my life.

'This isn't so bad,' I said to my pocket, where Susan Rabbit was tucked up next to a photograph of me with Mother, Father and Liffy, taken on my last short leave home.

But that feeling wouldn't last. After just ten minutes in the air, Sergeant Jim Glover, our nose-gunner yelled out, 'Enemy plane ahead!'

It was nothing but a dot on the horizon to begin with. I radioed through to base and was told the plane we'd seen wasn't on its own. A fact which soon became horrifically clear and frightening.

The rat-a-tat-a-tat of machine gun fire echoed through the sky around us as the Italian Regia Aeronautica attacked the Wellington in front of ours, piloted by Ronnie Hewitt. Hewitt's crew shot back and caught the Italian wing. Fire and Smoke billowed out and the plane tilted and fell into the ocean.

'Good riddance!' Sheepy cheered as the plane went down.

As we flew over, the smoke blocked my view, but coming out the other side I could see Ronnie's plane and breathed a sigh of relief. They were still ok.

With the relief came a stab of guilt for the fallen Italian pilot. He may have been our enemy and I was definitely grateful it was his plane that had gone down rather than Ronnie's. But he was still somebody's son, husband, brother, father or possibly all of those.

There wasn't time to worry about the lost pilot as I had to radio the details of the attack back.

'We've got more company,' yelled Jim as more Regia Aeronautica planes came out of the blue. This was the first air combat I'd seen and it turned into a dogfight. Italian planes were joined by German Messershmitts, decorated with fearsome, fanged faces.

'The blighters are everywhere,' said Sheepy. 'Fire back but choose your shots boys. We have limited ammunition to protect ourselves and once that's spent we'll be nothing more than sitting ducks.'

We had no choice but to fight back, and I was grateful to be at the radio rather than manning the guns. I knew it was bound to happen one day but this, my first taste of real warfare, I was glad to focus on the click click of Morse Code.

I saw planes fall. Both enemy and our own. My knuckles ached as I gripped the clicker and drummed out the messages from our plane as quickly as I could. Jellicoe was concentrating hard, navigating us towards Malta.

And then we saw the island. A very welcome sight despite the enemy planes still attacking. However, fate hadn't finished with us yet.

'We're short on fuel,' said Sheepy. 'We've got enough to get us down but it might be bumpy.'

I peeked at the gauge and saw that we were dangerously low. I wasn't sure whether we had enough to get us safely to the runway whilst still having to play dodge the bullet. But as we approached Malta we had friends on our side. Suddenly the planes I could see were not just those of the enemy.

'Hurricanes!' Sheepy shouted. 'They'll see us in.'

Our boys based on Malta had sent a welcoming party of Hurricane fighter planes to take the heat away from us and they were a sight for our sore eyes. With more craft joining in the dog fight, we were able to focus on getting to Malta. The longer we were in the sky, the more precious fuel we were using up and I was petrified it would run out before we made it to land.

Sweat found its way into my eyes but I couldn't let go of my clicker to lift my goggles and wipe it away. The smell of burning was all around and the noise was unlike anything I'd heard before. As we neared the island the sound of the engines and constant gun fire was joined by something else. Huge booming blasts that shook the skies, threatening to shake us all into the sea below.

'Anti-aircraft guns,' Sheepy said. 'They're really giving Hitler and Mussolini's chaps hell.'

Despite the Hurricanes and anti-aircraft guns, I couldn't share Sheepy's clear delight. Not until I could finally see the runway of Luqa Airbase in front of us. It was mercifully clear as Sheepy began a desperate descent on the vapours of fuel left in the tank. The landing wasn't graceful. We hit the ground and bounced but the plane stayed on her wheels and screeched to a halt. I closed my eyes and took a couple of deep breaths, almost as though I needed to fill my lungs in order to reassure my body that I had survived.

'Quick,' shouted a man, running up. 'Get out and we'll get her off the runway ready for the next plane coming in behind you.'

'We did as we were told and left the Wellie in safe hands.

'This way,' said another chap.

43

I ran after him as well as I could on my shaky legs and we were led away from the runway and into the heart of the airbase.

'What a welcome,' I said.

'Apparently our navy scrambled the German signals so they didn't know you were on your way. Otherwise, the carrier you came in on would almost certainly have been hit,' said the man who'd brought us in.

'Well, they certainly seemed to make up for it,' said Sheepy. 'I'm going to find the Squadron Leader. Find out which of our chaps made it down safely.'

'Rickson and Jarvis are over there,' said Jim Glover and he and the other gunners went over to shake hands with friends who'd landed just before us.

'First dog fight?' asked the man.

'Yes,' I said.

'You'll get used to it I'm afraid. Life here on Malta is all air raids and dog fights. Sorry, I'm Albert Powell, Albie. Been here almost two months now.'

He held out his hand and I shook it.

'John Hallett,' I said. 'And this is Flight Sergeant Jellicoe Hyde.'

'Welcome to Malta,' said Albie warmly. 'Come on, I'll show you where to sign in and find your digs. It's not too bad but don't expect luxury. Water and electricity are rationed out here just like the food. Can't even flush the toilet when you've been for a tinkle.'

As we crossed the room Sheepy joined us.

'I saw Frank Moraes, looking rather shocked,' he said. 'He told me John Cross and Ronnie Hewitt's planes were shot down. All crewmen lost.'

My mouth felt as dry as the Mediterranean summer air and my eyes prickled as though someone had blown sand into them. I had known this would happen of course. There was not even a tiny hope that every single man, every friend had been spared. The thought of these brave men who I'd shared my life with until a couple of hours ago, now lying at the bottom of the sea so far from home made it seem real for the first time.

'Bad luck,' Albie said. 'I'm afraid round here we get a bit too used to losing friends to Gerry. It doesn't make it any easier though when it happens.'

* * *

Later that evening, once we'd had a quick wash and been shown to our bunks, Jellicoe and I met up with the rest of our squadron in the mess for our first meal at Luqa airbase.

Albie was already there with some friends of his and he waved us over.

'Peter, Charlie Boy, meet John and Jelly,' he said. 'Just landed today.'

We all shook hands.

'It's Jellicoe,' Jellicoe said. 'Not Jelly.'

Charlie laughed. 'Well, if you insist on coming here with your fancy foreign name, don't expect folk to use it.'

Jellicoe frowned and Albie looked a bit taken about.

'Sorry,' he said. 'I'm sure Charlie didn't meant any harm. It's just we don't have many chaps from Africa here.'

'I'm from Jamaica,' said Jellicoe.

'Oh,' said Albie. 'Fair enough then, Jellicoe.'

His smile was warm and seemed genuine. I had to remind myself that the colour ban had only been lifted a couple of years earlier so Jellicoe's dark skin would cause heads to turn in Malta, just as they had when he arrived in RAF Hartwell. But he'd quickly proven himself to be hard working, funny and exceptionally kind. He was well respected and admired back home and I knew he'd settle into RAF Luqa just as quickly.

It didn't take long before Charlie, Peter and Albie were swapping stories with Jellicoe and I as easily as if we'd known each other for years. It was the beginning of a long camaraderie that would see us all through a lot of hard times to come.

CHAPTER 7

Eliza tried to imagine what it must have been like for John, flying into Malta under fire and then finding out that not everyone had made it safely. It made her think about Anaya. How would she feel if she never saw her again and hadn't taken her chance to say sorry and make up. Eliza knew the summer would be so much better with her friend in it and all the reasons for not going round to see her suddenly seemed unimportant. More than that, they were ridiculous.

'Come on Boo,' she called, taking his lead out of the chest by the front door. 'I'm just going round to Anaya's,' she shouted into the kitchen.

'Good decision,' Ganny cheered from the breakfast table where she was finishing off her porridge. 'That's my girl.'

Eliza blew her three kisses and Ganny caught them and threw three more back. Eliza waved and clipped the lead on Boo who was itching to get out and stretch his doggy legs.

The air felt summery and the blue sky looked happy as Eliza walked down the road to Anaya's house. Boo's claws clicked on the pavement and they had to stop several times for him to sniff fences, patches of dandelions and interesting bits of the kerb. Each time he managed to squeeze out a few drops of pee, just to let other dogs know he'd been there.

'Better a drip than nothing at all, hey Boo?' Eliza told him.

It was something Mum had always said, when she still used to go on walks with them.

Boo's tail started wagging as Eliza pushed open the little gate and walked into Anaya's front garden.

'You know where we are, don't you?' said Eliza. 'You're lucky Anaya's mum lets you come round still after you dug up all her daffodils. It's a good thing you're so adorable and everyone loves you.'

Eliza rang the doorbell and waited for the inevitable sound of chaos as Anaya's twin brothers Aadi and Devi raced each other to be the first to get there. But the house stayed quiet. She rang the bell again and knocked for good measure, just in case it wasn't working properly. Still no answer.

Eliza stepped back and looked at the house. All the curtains were drawn shut which was strange for that time in the morning.

'If you've looking for the Khatris,' said a lady leaning over the fence from her house next door. 'They've gone away for the summer I'm afraid. Niket and Rashmi have taken the children to her mum's for the summer. She's not too well and they're going to look after her.'

Eliza frowned.

'To India?' she said.

'That's right,' the next-door neighbour said. 'They had to go quite suddenly I think. Poor Rashmi, she's so worried about her mother. She popped in yesterday with a key for me so I can look after the house and water the plants. Such lovely plants she has.'

The woman kept talking but Eliza had stopped listening. How could Anaya have left for India without telling her? And then she remembered. Anaya *had* come round. But Eliza had refused to see her. No wonder she hadn't tried again. And her Granny was poorly too. Eliza wished more than anything that she'd been a better friend. Not been such an idiot about the boarding school business and been there for Anaya when she needed her.

'...and the roses,' the lady next door was saying. 'Nobody grows roses like Rashmi. They smell so wonderful that it's always a pleasure to sit out in my back garden in the summer and breathe them in.'

Eliza couldn't have been less interested in Mrs Khatri's roses.

'Sorry,' she said. 'I have to go home.'

As soon as she got home, Eliza took her phone from the drawer where she had hidden it when she hadn't wanted to talk to anyone. The battery was flat and when she plugged the charger in she saw there were three missed calls and two messages from Anaya. She read the first message.

Hi. Sorry you're not well. Hope you get better soon.
I'm sorry if I upset you. I didn't mean to.
  You're my best friend. Love A xxx

Eliza gulped back her tears and read the second message.

I got to go to India. My Granny's ill. If you feel ok, can

I come and see you before I go? We have to go early tomorrow to catch our plane. I miss you. A xxx

PS My phone won't work in India. Too expensive so I hope you call me today.

Eliza felt as though someone had reached into her belly and scooped everything out, leaving her hollow. She tried calling Anaya even though she knew it would go straight to answerphone. She sent a message and wondered how long it would be before Anaya could read it. Would it be too late to mend their friendship by then?

I know it's too late but I wanted to say sorry. Really really sorry.

I hope your Granny is okay. I wish I hadn't switched off my phone and that I had come to the door when you came round.

You're my best friend too and I really miss you
E xxx

'How was Anaya?' Ganny asked when Eliza went downstairs.

'She wasn't in,' said Eliza.

'Not to worry. You can always try again later.'

'She won't be back until the end of the summer,' Eliza said. Her shoulders felt saggy and her head felt heavy. She went and sat next to Ganny and rested her head on the back of the sofa. Ganny leant back too so their heads were just touching on the cushions.

'I see,' said Ganny. 'That's terribly rough luck.'

Once again tears sprung into Eliza's eyes.

'Oh, Poppet,' said Ganny. 'I know it's hard but there will

be plenty of time to make things right again when she's home.'

Eliza shook her head. 'She'll be going off to her fancy ballet boarding school,' she whispered.

'Oh now,' said Ganny. 'That sounds tricky for you.'

Eliza nodded.

'But awfully exciting for her,' Ganny said gently.

'Yes.'

'Was that what you argued about?'

'Yes,' said Eliza. 'Mostly that. And I never said sorry to her.'

Ganny rubbed Eliza's knee. 'She'll understand. Trust me, real friends always understand and if there's one thing I can whole-heartedly say about Anaya, it's that she is a very real friend.'

At that moment Boo came bounding into the room and straight over to the empty armchair. His tail was wagging like a windscreen wiper in the heaviest rainstorm.

'Boo!' exclaimed Eliza. 'What's got into you?'

He flipped over onto his back and aimed his tummy at the chair.

'If you want it tickled, you'd better come over here,' said Eliza. 'There's nobody in that chair.'

But Boo looked perfectly happy, stretched out on his back where he was. Eliza looked at Boo, then the chair and then at Ganny. She was watching the dog with a smile on her face.

Eliza found herself staring at the chair then, searching for any sign that anyone was there. She realised she was hoping to see John, sitting in the chair scratching Boo on the tummy.

Don't be daft she said to herself, *ghosts don't exist.*

* * *

Later that evening, Mum crept into Eliza's room to say goodnight.

'I'm sorry I missed dinner again,' she said. 'Work's so busy at the moment that I feel like I hardly get to see you these days.'

'It's fine,' said Eliza.

'Things will settle down I promise,' said Mum. 'Why don't we book in a day for the two of us to spend some quality time together? Do something special, just us.'

'Yes please,' said Eliza. 'Saturday?'

'We'll see,' Mum smiled, brushing the hair out of Eliza's eyes. 'Ganny told me about Anaya going away. I'm sorry about that.'

Eliza shrugged.

'You're welcome to have other friends over this summer. Whenever you like.'

'Don't worry,' said Eliza. 'I've got Ganny.'

'You two really are peas in a pod,' Mum said. 'It was a very good decision to name you after her. My two favourite Elizabeths.'

'You love Ganny too, don't you?'

'What a silly question,' Mum said, looking shocked. 'Of course I do. When I was your age I spent almost all my time with Ganny. Mum – your Granny P – was always off for weekends away or on dates or days out. I don't think she was a natural mother but Ganny was always there for me. She's one of a kind.'

Mum bent down so she could whisper in Eliza's ear.

'My biggest secret, something I've never told anyone before, not even Dad, is that I loved Ganny more than I loved my own mother. Is that terrible?'

'No,' said Eliza. She didn't add that she wondered if she might be feeling the same about Ganny and Mum these days.

'If you love her so much,' she said instead. 'Why are you sending her away?'

'What?' Mum asked.

'I saw all the brochures. You know for the care homes.'

Mum took a deep breath.

'Nothing has been decided,' she said. 'We're just looking at all our options.'

'But you just said you loved Ganny,' Eliza said, sitting up in bed. 'So how could you even be thinking about it? She belongs here.'

'Ganny's old, Eliza,' said Mum. 'She sometimes falls over and there isn't always someone here to help get her back on her feet.'

'She's only fallen down once or twice,' Eliza half shouted. 'I fall down all the time. Are you going to pack me off to some home as well?'

'Eliza!'

'I won't ever speak to you again if you send Ganny away.'

Eliza could feel her eyes blazing and her face prickling from the heat of her anger.

'Listen,' Mum tried.

'No,' said Eliza. 'I'm going to sleep.'

She threw herself back down and pulled her pillow over her head. After a short while, she peeked out and found that Mum had left and closed the bedroom door behind her.

Eliza clenched her teeth and balled her fists tightly. Then she found her fists were pumping at her pillow, hitting and thumping in frustration and hurt. And she cried. For Ganny and for Anaya. The two people who meant most to her and who were both going to be taken away. And then for John and for the friends he'd lost as they flew into Malta. She cried and cried until her pillow was soaked and her eyes felt as though someone had rubbed them dry with sandpaper.

Sleep was as far away from her as Anaya was so Eliza took out her tiny reading torch and opened Ganny's journal.

CHAPTER 8

MALTA - SEPTEMBER 1941

Malta took a mighty battering in those terrible months. It was bombed daily, often three times a day. For such a small island, it was a vital pawn in the war and the people living there wore this role that had been thrust upon them with courage and grit like I'd never seen before.

On a rare day off, Jellicoe, Albie and I decided to leave Luqa airbase and take bikes into Valletta, the tiny capital of the island, to get a change of scene. I'd been before when I'd been sent to Grand Harbour to assist with the unloading of one of the very few supply ships that made it through the AXIS defence. But it had changed a lot since then.

'Goodness,' I said as we walked through the enormous piles of rubble. 'I thought London had it bad but here there's hardly anything left standing.'

A woman and her young daughter, both covered in white limestone dust, were picking through the rubble. The mother was chattering away in Maltese but the daughter said nothing.

'Trying to find whatever they can salvage of their possessions,' Albie said. 'Poor blighters.'

Outside the remains of a hollowed-out shop someone had set up a stall and was selling vegetables grown on the local farms. A queue snaked up the street as people handed over their ration slips and chose their tiny supply of fruit and vegetables.

'It's amazing how many smiles you see,' Jellicoe pointed out. 'If you look for them.'

'You're right,' I said, looking around me. Mingled in with the utter destruction and heart-breaking chaos, people still found the power to smile at each other, hug their families and chat with their neighbours.

'They're a lesson in resilience alright Jellicoe my friend,' said Albie. 'A lesson none of us will ever forget, I'm sure.'

At that moment, the unmistakable shriek of the air raid sirens pierced the air and Valletta became a buzz of action as everyone made for the caves and passages, hacked into the limestone under the town. Jellicoe, Albie and I followed and joined a crush of people in a large cave lined with metal bunks where people could sleep if the raids continued.

'Look at that,' Albie nudged my arm and nodded at a family huddled in one corner. They'd set up camp and it looked as though they'd been there for quite some time judging by the way they'd organised their few belongings.

'Lots of people live down here,' Jellicoe said. 'If they've lost their home and they've nowhere else to go they sleep down here, cook, wash, everything.'

I breathed in the dank, musty air that smelled of a hundred dirty armpits. I thought our cramped quarters back at Luqa were bad enough, but this? These terrible, squalid conditions were absolutely no place to be living. But what choice did they have?

I gasped loudly as the cave shook from the force of an explosion outside. Lime dust peppered us from above but the solid stone stood firm, keeping us safe. Another blast, this time even closer. I felt chunks of rock, dislodged from the ceiling of the cave, fall into my hair. My ears rang and I could see children crying and frightened parents trying to comfort them.

Another explosion, further away now but still loud enough to set my teeth chattering. I looked at Jellicoe. He was grim-faced and I knew he was thinking the same as I was. Would these people live to see peace on their island? Would any of us?

The air raid was a mercifully short one and we were all very happy to get above ground again. The air was thick with dust as we walked away from the shelter. It clogged my nose and throat and I had to squint to stop it getting into my eyes.

Near the edge of the city, where the dust had started to settle, we came across a boy no older than four or five, sitting on a pile of fallen stones and sobbing his little heart out. There was nobody else around so we went over to see if we could help.

'What's the matter?' Jellicoe asked gently.

The boy looked at him with big red eyes.

'Tlift lil omm,'[1] he said.

'I don't speak your language,' Jellicoe said. He looked back at Albie and I but neither of us could help.

'Omm, Ommi,'[2] the little boy said and started to cry again.

'Where are your parents?' I asked slowly. 'Your mother? Father?'

'Fejn hi Ommi?'[3] he asked, sniffing,

'I think he's all on his tod, poor mite,' said Albie.

'Luca!' called a woman, hurrying down the lane with her arms wide open. 'It-tarbija tieghi, Luca.'[4]

The boy, Luca, stumbled and tripped his way toward her as quickly as he could.

'OMMI!!' he shouted as he flung himself into her open arms.

I didn't need to understand Maltese to understand that a mother had just found the son she obviously thought she'd lost to the raid.

* * *

Back at the airbase, Jellicoe, Albie and I hardly spoke a word to each other. We'd all seen a lot of destruction since coming to Malta, but there was something different about witnessing the air raid at Valletta. These people hadn't asked to be tangled up in the war. And yet thousands of

_____
1   I lost my mother.
2   Mum, mummy.
3   Where's my mother?
4   My baby

families were paying so very dearly for living in a place of such great importance.

Malta was the gateway to the much-needed oil supplies of the Suez Canal and the Middle East. Strategically vital but to the Maltese it was home. A home that was being destroyed at a terrifying rate in front of their eyes.

'Come on old chap,' Albie said, giving me a poke in the ribs. 'Not often we get the whole day off. I challenge you to a game of cards. Jellicoe, how about you? Are you in?'

'Am I in?' Jellicoe chuckled. 'You give me any opportunity to beat this skinny British man and I am always most certainly in.'

'Beat me?' I laughed back. 'Oh, I think not old chum. However I accept your challenge and look forward to making you eat your words.'

So the three of us sat in the mess, listening to the buzz of aircraft flying overhead and the boom of the powerful anti-aircraft guns. We played whist and gin rummy and we tried to pretend, just for a few hours, that life was normal and we were three friends without a care in the world, enjoying each other's company.

CHAPTER 9

Eliza sat in the bath feeling stupid. Ganny had taught her to count up her blessings whenever she had an attack of the glums. Sometimes this helped a lot, but not this time. This time if anything it made her feel worse.

She couldn't stop thinking about the little boy in the rubble, and all those people in Malta who had lost their homes. Jellicoe had pointed out that they still managed to smile and if they could do it then what right did she have to be so gloomy? She had a really comfy, easy life compared to them.

Eliza got out of the bath and towelled herself dry. It was a hot day so she left her hair damp and pulled on an old T-shirt and her short dungarees. Ganny was always saying that fresh air and nature were the best tonics so Eliza decided to give it a try.

There were some places Eliza was allowed to walk on her own – as long as she took her phone with her, and some places she wasn't. The golf course was fine, the park was fine, the edge of the woods was fine. But the paths that led further into the woods were not allowed and the chalk quarry was a definite no go.

Eliza was bored of the park so she turned left at the end of her street and crossed over to the back of the golf course. Boo was supposed to be kept on his lead but there was nobody playing golf and Boo always came when she called him so Eliza decided to let him off for a proper run.

'We can always clip it back on you if we meet anyone,' she said.

'I do that too,' a voice behind said, making her jump.

'Sorry,' said a boy about the same age as her. He was wearing a big baggy green jumper and jeans even though the sun was hotter than it had been all year.

'I'm Jonathan,' the boy said. 'But most people just call me Jonno.'

'You've got a Jack Russell too,' Eliza said, looking down at the little dog that was running with Boo in excited circles.

'She's called Scout,' Jonno said. 'What's yours called?'

'Boo,' said Eliza.

'Brilliant,' said Jonno. 'Like the book.'

'What?' said Eliza.

'Scout and Boo. They're both in To Kill a Mockingbird.'

'I haven't read that,' said Eliza.

'We had to at school,' said Jonno. 'What year are you?'

'After the summer I'll be going into Year 7,' said Eliza.

'Cool,' said Jonno. 'Just one year below me. Mind if I walk with you? Scout seems to be pretty keen on Boo.'

Eliza nodded. She'd gone out to find peace and space to think but actually it might be nice to have some company for a change.

'Do you live around here then?' Jonno asked.

'Yeah,' Eliza said. 'Just the other side of the park.'

'Cool,' said Jonno. 'I live in Manchester but I'm staying with my Grandma for the summer.'

They walked close to the hedgerow at the edge of the golf course with Boo and Scout running rings around them and each other. Eliza lost track of the time as they wandered up and down the grassy verge. She absentmindedly tugged stems of cow parsley from the overgrown wildness that grew next to the hedges and twisted them into knots.

'What did they do to you?' Jonno asked.

'What?' Eliza asked.

'The flowers that you're ripping to bits.'

'Oh,' said Eliza. Looking at the mangled stalk and then throwing it back into the hedgerow.

'I like this part of the golf course best of all,' she said. 'Much nicer than the fancy cut grass where they play.'

'Definitely,' said Jonno. 'Much better.'

'How come you're here for the whole summer?' Eliza asked. 'Did your family come too?'

'Just my little brother and me,' said Jonno. 'Mum and Dad are too busy with work to look after us.'

'I know the feeling,' said Eliza. 'It's sometimes like they've forgotten they have me in my house.'

'Parents, hey?' shrugged Jonno.

'Parents!' Eliza agreed. She didn't know why, but hearing Jonno talk about his parents made her feel just a little bit better about her own.

'Sometimes I wonder if I actually even like mine,' Jonno admitted. 'Not Mum so much but Dad makes it pretty difficult. He's always yelling and shouting at us. I can't do anything right no matter how hard I try. So, I don't try any more. Maybe that's why they sent me here for the summer.'

He stopped and grinned at Eliza. 'Whoa, I can't believe I just said that. I must have been bottling it up ready so I could dump it all on someone I only met about...' he glanced at his watch, 'an hour and a half ago!'

Eliza grinned back. It felt nice that someone trusted her enough to tell her such important things.

'How old's your brother?' she asked.

'He's nine,' Jonno said. 'And a right pain in the bum. Always whinging and complaining about everything. If we have a fight, Mum and Dad always take his side because he shouts louder so it's easier for them if he gets his own way.'

'I always wanted a brother,' said Eliza. 'But now, maybe I'm glad I don't.'

'Is it just you and your mum and dad then?'

'And Ganny,' said Eliza. 'She's my great-gran and she lives with us.'

'Cool,' said Jonno.

'Yeah, she is,' said Eliza. 'It's brilliant having her with us. But Mum's trying to put her in a home.'

'Really?' said Jonno.

'Mum says it's for the best but I think that's rubbish. I think it's just easier for them to have her in a home so they don't have to worry about her.'

Eliza wasn't exactly sure why but she found herself opening up to Jonno about everything then. This strange boy in the green jumper that she'd only just met, listened as she told him about Ganny and how much she loved having her around. Then she told him about Anaya and their row.

About Amy and school and how Eliza always felt as though she was on the edge of everything.

'Anaya's my only friend really,' she surprised herself by admitting.

'Except for Boo here,' Jonno said.

'Of course,' said Eliza.

She was suddenly shy.

'Now I'm the one who's over-shared,' she said.

'We're even then,' Jonno grinned. 'I think they're all muppets. I've only been your friend for a bit and I already think you're pretty cool.'

'Thanks,' said Eliza blushing a little.

'Wait til you get to secondary school though,' he said. 'I didn't know anyone when I started. Well not unless you count Reuben Fellows who I went to primary with but who always called me Jona-thong and tried to give me wedgies.'

'He sounds like a real idiot,' said Eliza.

'Yeah,' said Jonno. 'But I met loads of kids who weren't idiots. After the first term I had lots of friends.'

'But you're easy to talk to,' Eliza pointed out. 'I'm the total opposite.'

'No you're not,' said Jonno. 'You're the first person I've told about my mum and dad.'

'Oh,' said Eliza.

They walked on for a bit, each thinking their own thoughts. Then Jonno stopped suddenly and punched his arm in the air.

'I've got it!' he said.

'Got what?' asked Eliza.

'Got a plan to stop your parents sending your Granny away.'

'Go on,' said Eliza.

'If they're sending her away to make their lives easier, then we find loads of different ways to show how important she is. All the things she does to help out.'

'Brilliant idea!' said Eliza. 'Like mending things, cooking dinner, babysitting me. Not that I need babysitting anymore but, you know...'

'Worth adding it to the list,' agreed Jonno.

As they got back to the path Eliza needed to take to go back home, she was sad to say goodbye to her new friend but too shy to ask if they could meet up again.

'I haven't seen you on the golf course before,' she said.

'I usually walk in the woods,' said Jonno. 'Scout likes chasing squirrels and rabbits and the woods are full of them. We could go there tomorrow if you like?'

Eliza was about to say that she wasn't really allowed far into the woods when she was out on her own. But then she thought that if she was with Jonno and Scout then she wasn't technically on her own, was she?

'Yeah, sure,' she said. She took out her phone. 'Shall I text you when I get there?'

'Wow,' said Jonno. 'Is that your phone?'

Eliza looked at the ancient hand-me-down of Dad's with the cracked screen.

'I was hoping for an upgrade for my birthday,' she said. 'But I got a new coat instead.'

'It looks amazing,' said Jonno. 'I don't even have a phone. So, let's just say we'll meet by the path at the back of the park at ten tomorrow?'

'Great,' said Eliza.

'Cool,' said Jonno. 'See you tomorrow.'

The weight on Eliza's shoulders was hardly there as she made her way back home. Jonno was right, she would just have to prove to Mum and Dad how important Ganny was and then they'd HAVE to let her stay. And Jonno, her new friend, was going to help her.

CHAPTER 10

MALTA – OCTOBER 1941

I was glad when the heat of summer eased a little as autumn took hold. Apart from the constant mosquitoes and the sweaty horror of our uniforms when it was almost forty degrees in the sun, flying was so much trickier in the heat. Hot pockets of air swirled over the island making the planes do funny, unexpected things in the turbulence.

I had grown oddly used to life at Luqa despite the constant attacks from Germany and Italy and the dangerous missions we were sent on. I never got used to those.

I missed home terribly of course, it was so far away and life couldn't have been more different if I'd actually gone to live on the moon instead of Malta. But we all just got on with it. I suppose we didn't really have a choice. Jellicoe, Albie and the other chaps made things easier. It's hard to explain the strength of the friendships that are created when you are thrown together in such strange and dangerous times. It meant that every man we lost was like losing a member of the family though, which was incredibly tough.

'Out of bed lazy man,' Jellicoe said, pulling the blankets off my bunk. 'There's work to be done.'

'I was having such a lovely dream,' I complained, trying to tug my blankets back.

'Was I in it?' he grinned.

'Yes,' I said. 'You were in a boat about to tumble over the edge of a very high waterfall.'

Jellicoe's throaty chuckle was infectious and I smiled.

'If I ever find myself in that position, you know I'd hit the water at the bottom and just go right on paddling,' he said.

'Jellicoe, I don't doubt that for a second. You're like a cat with nine lives.'

'More like a tiger with ninety.'

'I do hope so old chap. I hope we both are.'

When we went into the mess for breakfast, there was much excitement as a rare delivery of letters from home had managed to get through. I crossed my fingers and prayed hard and it worked! My envelope contained three letters, from Mother, Father and Liffy. Just holding those little scraps of home in my hands took me straight back to my family. I could almost smell Mother's cooking and Father's pipe tobacco. And I could hear Liffy's laughter so clearly that it made me smile at the thousands of jokes we'd shared.

'Enjoy your letters,' Jellicoe said. 'I'm going to take a copy of the Times of Malta and see what's what.'

He took the daily newspaper and gave me a little space to read my precious post. Mother's news was mainly about the village whilst Father proudly told me about the great effort he and the rest of the Home Guard were doing. Liffy wanted me to know about her rise up the ranks of the tennis club as well as all the knitting she was doing with the WI. I drank in every word they wrote, savouring them and filing away their news. But when I got to the end of Liffy's letter, I read an added footnote so dreadful that I had to clamp my teeth together for fear of vomiting up the single slice of bread and butter I'd been given for breakfast.

Oh John, she wrote.

The most terrible news. Mr Chandler has just called round. Mummy says that I shouldn't tell you but Daddy says that he's sure you'd want to know. I can hardly bear to write the words but here they are. Dearest Bill is missing. His ship was sunk near the coast of France and he wasn't amongst the crew rescued. They are assuming the worst and we're all so desperately gloomy as I know you will be. I'm sending you so much love and wish for your return to us soon. Don't forget to keep Susan Rabbit safely in your pocket.

Liffy xxx

I laid the sheets of paper on the table and stared at them. All I could think about was Bill. The last time I'd seen him and the terrible things I'd said when he told me he wasn't joining the RAF with me. And now he was gone.

'Alright old man?' Sheepy asked, pulling up a chair next to mine.

'Not really,' I confessed. 'Not great news from home.'

'Sorry to hear that,' Sheepy said. 'Chin up though, I'm afraid we've been called up for a mission. Seems Gerry is trying to sneak tankers to North Africa and we can't let them get through and refuel their troops can we now? Eh?'

'No Sir,' I said.

'Good. Come with me. Flight Sergeant Hyde, you too. Albright and McHugh will man the guns, nose and tail. I don't think we can spare a third gunner at the waist, but you can assist if needed can't you, Hallett? Hopefully we can sweep in, Hyde will drop the bombs and we can be out of there without getting involved in any dog-fighting.'

'Yes Sir,' I said.

'Very good,' Sheepy said. 'Look sharp, kit up and be ready in five minutes on the strip.'

'Yes Sir,' I said again.

Pushing thoughts of Bill aside wasn't as hard as it might have been as there was no time really to think of anything other than the mission ahead. I was glad Jellicoe was to navigate us. There was no better navigator than Flight Sergeant Jellicoe Hyde. Together we grabbed our kit and ran onto the airstrip where we found Sheepy already in the cockpit of the Wellington bomber. We pulled on our yellow life jackets and parachutes, climbed aboard and took our positions.

The two gunners had already done the same and Sheepy started the engine.

'Chocks away,' he yelled above the roar of the engines and we began to hurtle down the runway. I knew how to pilot a plane myself but I'd only every flown Hurricanes and other smaller single man planes as part of my training, never a Wellington.

We were soon in the air, every man focussed on their task, heading once more into the skies. I concentrated on the radio and relayed information to Sheepy.

'Skies all clear Sir,' I said

'Just the way we like them hey, Hallett!'

We flew for about fifteen minutes with Jellicoe giving clear instructions to locate the German tanker.

'There she is,' McHugh called out from his observation point as nose gunner.

I tapped out the message that we had spotted the ship.

'Right you are,' answered Sheepy.

The tanker had anti-aircraft guns attached to protect her and these started firing as soon as we were close enough. I patted my pocket and was grateful to know Susan Rabbit was safely there, bringing us all luck.

'Target in range,' Jellicoe shouted.

'Fire when ready,' Sheepy commanded, and Jellicoe released the bomb.

Sheepy ramped up to full throttle as we sped away to a safe distance. The boom of the bomb as it hit the tanker was awful and I tried not to think of the terrified crew onboard.

'We need to release the second,' said Sheepy. 'Now, whilst the smoke is hindering their gunners.'

We circled around for the second attack, all the while I was letting base know what we were doing.

The second bomb hit and we dropped a third. This time, the blast of the bomb was followed by another one, ten or even twenty times as big. Flames shot high into the sky and we found ourselves in a phenomenal smoke cloud.

'I'd say that'd do it,' said Sheepy. 'Must have ignited the fuel they were carrying. Poor devils were sitting on a bomb much bigger than anything we could have dropped on them.'

I knew it had to happen. I also knew that, in the end, it would have been a pretty quick death for everyone on board. But I couldn't stop thinking about poor Bill. We'd just sunk a whole ship load of people just like him.

'Target destroyed,' I clicked back to base. 'Target destroyed. Mission successful. Heading back to base.'

I was glad of my flying mask as we flew back to Luqa. Glad of the barrier it put between my tears and all of those who might question them.

'Damn Gerry,' yelled McHugh. 'They're onto us sir. Two heading our way.'

'Hallett,' Sheepy shouted. 'Take position as waist gunner. Looks like we're going to need you after all.'

My heart sank. This was the first time I had been called to man the gun and I felt terrified at the power I held in my hands. But there was no choice and no time to think too much about it. The rat-a-tat of our guns filled the plane as we tried to defend ourselves so that Sheepy could bring us down safely. I lined up one of the planes in my sight and shot back, desperately pushing away the unhelpful thoughts of the lives inside the planes I was trying to destroy.

Suddenly, a tremendous crash shook the plane and we lurched over to the left. The smell of burning filled my nostrils and a red glow lit up the air around us.

'We're hit,' Sheepy said. 'I can't control her. Bail out crew. That's an order.'

Jellicoe wrenched off the door and looked around him.

'Albright,' he said. 'Jump!'

Sergeant Albright didn't need to be told twice. He jumped clean out of the plane and was followed quickly by McHugh.'

'Sir!' I called.

'I need to take her as far out to sea as I can,' Sheepy yelled. 'We've still got three explosives on board. If we crash on landing it'll be a disaster. Now go.'

'But sir,' I said, knowing the danger he was putting himself in.

'Jump now, Hallett. That's an order.'

So, I did.

Looking down, I could see the two parachutes of Albright and McHugh. I pulled my own cord when I was clear of the plane and prayed that Jellicoe had jumped right behind me.

There was nothing else I could do except watch as Flight Lieutenant Elmer Mutton, Sheepy, took the plane out to sea and gave up his own life in order to save countless others.

I was so overcome with the events of that terrible day that I forgot to watch my landing. I hit the ground with a crump and immediately I blacked out.

CHAPTER 11

Eliza's heart was in her mouth as she turned the pages. She knew things like this had happened, but to read about someone in her own family and put names and a story to the people it had happened to was completely different. Poor Bill, sinking with his ship. And brave, incredible Sheepy.

'Knock knock,' Ganny said as she pushed Eliza's door open.

'Oh Ganny,' said Eliza. 'Bill!'

'You're reading John's story.' Ganny looked really pleased.

'And poor Sheepy.'

'Yes indeed,' said Ganny. 'He saved John's life that day. And who knows how many others.'

'And you were back home not knowing what was happening to him.'

'That was the worst part,' said Ganny. 'The not knowing of it all. But we kept ourselves busy enough.'

'Making socks with your mum and putting out fires with your dad,' Eliza said.

'It was just like that magnet your mum keeps on the fridge. We kept calm and we carried on.'

'It must have been so hard for you when Bill's ship sank.'

Ganny's face crumpled as her mind took her back to that painful time.

'I remember the day poor Mr Chandler came round. He'd always been a sickly-looking man but that day he looked more like a skeleton than a living person. Like the telegram had sucked all life out of him.'

Eliza gave her Ganny a hug. She had lived through so much and had known the pain of real hardship and loss.

'Thank you for letting me read the journal,' Eliza said.

'Thank you for reading it,' said Ganny. 'Now come on, I've been up for hours waiting for a game of Backgammon to start the day.'

'I'll just have a quick shower and then I'm definitely ready to beat you on the board,' said Eliza. 'But only for a game or two this morning because I'm going for a walk with a friend at ten o'clock.'

Ganny's little eyes wrinkled as her whole face smiled.

'What a lovely day for a walk,' she said. 'Anyone I know?'

'It's a new friend I met on the golf course yesterday. He's called Jonno and he's staying with his Grandma for the summer.'

'That's wonderful, Darling,' beamed Ganny.

'And he has a dog called Scout. Not any kind of dog either but a Jack Russell.'

'I like him already,' said Ganny. 'And maybe one day you'll let me meet him.'

'Definitely,' said Eliza. 'I'll ask if he wants to come round.'

'Excellent plan,' said Ganny. 'Now I'll go and set the board out whilst you have a wash.'

'Oh Ganny,' called Eliza, holding up three socks with holes in the heels. 'Is there any way you could mend these for me please? I don't know how I ended up with so many holes in my socks.'

'Of course I will,' said Ganny. 'But you'll have to pay me with char and chatter.'

Sharing a cup of tea and a chat with Ganny was definitely a good bargain so Eliza agreed.

Before she went into the bathroom for her shower, Eliza slipped into Mum and Dad's bedroom and opened Dad's sock drawer. Maybe some of his socks could do with holes to patch too.

* * *

Jonno and Scout were already on the path at the back of the park when Eliza and Boo arrived. She spotted his green jumper way before she was close enough to recognise his face.

'Sorry I'm late,' said Eliza.

Jonno looked at his watch. 'I make it 9:57,' he said. 'Which means you're not late. I am just nearly always early. I think we've lost the dogs already by the way.'

Eliza looked around and sure enough, there was no sign of Boo or Scout.

'Boo!' she called.

'Scout will have taken her into the woods,' said Jonno. 'Like I told you, she's always chasing after rabbits and squirrels.'

Boo's furry head popped out of the woods for a second to show that he'd heard Eliza but then he turned and ran straight back in again.

'We'd better follow,' said Jonno. 'Come on.'

The wood was lovely and cool and Eliza loved the way the sun shone through the bright green of the trees above them. It spotted the brown earth with little dabs of sunlight that managed to sneak through the gaps between the leaves.

'Have you ever been here when the bluebells are out?' she asked.

'Yes,' Jonno said. 'I always come here when I visit Grandma. I'll show you where I built my den last summer. It's off the path so nobody's knocked it down.'

They pushed through the tall ferns and climbed over fallen branches. Eliza's trainers filled with dusty earth and she scratched her bare arms several times. But when they got to Jonno's den, it was definitely worth it.

'Did you do this on your own?' she asked.

'Just me, Scout and this.' He pulled a red army knife from his pocket. 'It was my Grandad's.'

'Cool, isn't it?' said Jonno.

Eliza looked at the tent of thick branches and logs rising up from the green sea of ferns. All cleverly propped against each other, tied in places with thick rope. The rope had gone black and straggly from being outside but it was still holding the logs in place – just about.

'Wow!' she said. 'It's really brilliant.'

It was a lot bigger than she'd thought it would be. 'How do we get in?' she asked.

'Round the other side,' said Jonno. 'I'll show you.'

Eliza followed Jonno.

'You'll have to push the ferns away,' he said.

Eliza did what he said and found a gap in the logs, just big enough for her to squeeze through. Boo and Scout almost knocked her flying as they raced each other into the den. The logs looked sturdy but when she put her hand on one to steady herself, she was surprised at how spongy it felt.

'Haven't you pair heard of manners?' she said to the dogs.

Inside there was a piece of old kitchen flooring on the ground that was faded and covered in a green layer of something. It smelled damp and woody inside which Eliza thought was unsurprising considering they were in a den made of branches in the middle of the wood.

'We should patch up these holes,' she said, pointing to an area where the den had fallen away. 'Look, the wood's rotted, we should find some fresh branches. We could do that now, come and help me.'

She stood up to leave but Jonno stopped her. 'Not now,' he said. 'It can wait. I quite like it being a bit tumble down anyway. It makes me feel like an explorer who's stumbled on an old forgotten cave.'

A large log lay across the back of the den and Jonno went and sat down on it.

'You've even made a sofa,' said Eliza.

'Perfect for planning,' he said. 'Talking of which, how are you getting on with *Operation Save Ganny From the Old Fogies Home*?'

Eliza ran her hand over the log to get rid of the cobwebs. She sat down next to Jonno but a chunk of the rotting log came away under her and she ended up dropping to the ground with her legs out in front of her.

'Whoops,' said Jonno. 'Sit here instead.'

He stood up to make space.

'It's covered in cobwebs,' Eliza said.

'Not afraid of spiders, are you?' said Jonno.

'It's not that,' said Eliza. 'It's just weird that you managed to sit down and stay pretty clean but I have cobwebs all over me.'

'Didn't I tell you I've got a magical butt?' Jonno laughed.

'Don't be daft,' Eliza giggled back.'

'Back to the big op,' said Jonno. 'What have you done since yesterday?'

'I may accidentally have picked holes in three of my socks. And Dad might find that three of his have also got big holes in them when he goes to get a pair out tomorrow.'

Jonno rubbed his hands together and hunched his shoulders like he was seriously getting into the role of evil plotter.

'Excellent start,' he said. 'But we need to go bigger and better.'

'What do you suggest?'

'Does your Mum have a favourite jumper?'

Eliza thought about it for no more than two seconds.

'The blue and green fancy cardigan she bought in Italy,' she said. 'It's made from cashmere. I know this because she yelled at me when I borrowed it once and said that cashmere is really expensive. She only wears it whenever she has her really important meetings because it's the poshest thing she's got.'

'Perfect!' said Jonno. 'When you get home, you know what to do.'

'I certainly do!' grinned Eliza.

CHAPTER 12

MALTA — OCTOBER 1941

I came to with my right leg hooked painfully under my body and a crushing feeling in my chest. For a second or two I panicked, wondering where I was and what was covering me like a shroud. When my head cleared and I remembered the events that had put me in the furrowed field I was lying in, I understood that the fabric over me was, in fact, my parachute.

Untangling myself from the canopy was a painful task as every small movement sent shooting pains into my leg. Breathing was also a lot harder than it should have been but if I tried too hard to get air into my body, it felt as though somebody was thrusting knives into my chest.

'Hello?' a voice called and I felt the canopy lift as someone helped get me free of the yards and yards of silk fabric.

'You are hurt?' asked a girl around my age when I

was finally able to see who my rescuer was. She had huge eyes that had clearly seen much hardship but were so very generous in their sympathy.

'I think so,' I said. But talking made me wince and clutch my chest in pain.

'You are not, I think,' said the girl. 'You can move to my cart perhaps?'

I looked to where she pointed and I saw a farm cart pulled by a large but scrawny horse. The poor thing was clearly as underfed as the rest of us on the island.

I'm not sure how I managed but, with a lot of help from the girl, I dragged myself to the cart and up into the back where I collapsed with my face scrunched up and my teeth clenched against the excruciating pain in my leg.

'My name is Azalea,' the girl said. 'I take you to my grandfather and we help you.'

'You're very kind,' I replied. My crushed chest made any more conversation hard but Azalea seemed to understand this. She chatted softly to me to take my mind off the pain as we bumped over the plough furrows.

'My grandfather is farmer,' she explained. 'I live with him now. My parents not alive when our house... Pwoosh!'

She used her hands to demonstrate an explosion.

'I'm so sorry,' I said. It felt incredibly insufficient but I couldn't find any other words at that moment.

Azalea shrugged and gave a big sigh.

'We all have bad things,' she said. 'But we all help each other and we get to the end. One good day, we get to the end.'

* * *

If I hadn't been in so much pain I might have wondered about how Azalea's grandfather might react to her bringing an injured airman to his house but there was no need to worry.

'This is my grandfather, Maurice,' Azalea said.

He climbed up into the cart and looked gravely at me as Azalea spoke to him in Maltese. His hands on my chest were gentle and his voice soft as he opened my jacket to check my injuries.

He breathed out through his teeth, making a low whistle. He said something else to Azalea and then he swapped places with Azalea. Maurice clicked and the horse set off at a slow pace. Although we took it steady, the journey to Imtarfa where the 90th General Hospital was felt as though we were driving over deep ruts and cobblestones. Azalea sat in the cart with me. She had a cool cloth which she used to mop my forehead.

'No sleep John,' she said gently. 'You stay awake. We not be a long time, then a doctor will care for you.'

She held my hand as I listened to her talking. Focussing on her helped take my mind away from my breathing which was getting more and more difficult.

When we got to the hospital, I was put on a stretcher and had only just enough time to thank Azalea and Maurice quickly before I was whisked inside and patched up by a team of the most wonderful doctors and nurses. I was given something to knock me out and, when I came around, I was lying in a bed on a ward with a dozen or so other men.

'Welcome back Flight Sergeant Hallett,' said a nurse who was using the watch pinned to her apron to check my pulse. 'How are you feeling?'

'Woozy,' I said.

'That'll be the anaesthesia,' she said. 'It'll wear off soon enough. Here, sip some water.'

The water was warm but it felt good in my claggy mouth.

'Three cracked ribs and a punctured lung.' The nurse indicated the bandages wrapped tightly around my chest. 'To go with your fractured leg and dislocated knee. You're lucky the farmer and his grand-daughter found you and brought you in.'

And I knew I was lucky. Luckier than brave Sheepy who'd taken the Wellington down to save us. Luckier than Azalea who had lost both parents and her home. And luckier than Bill who'd been lost to us in the English Channel.

'Where's my uniform?' I asked.

'They had to cut your trousers off I'm afraid.'

'But my jacket?' I said. 'I had something important in the pocket.'

'I'll track it down for you,' said the nurse as she patted my hand. 'Now rest, if you can.'

I drifted in and out of fretful sleep. It sounds silly when compared to everything that was happening around me, but I couldn't stop thinking about Susan Rabbit. She was my link to home, to Liffy. She was also a symbol of hope and a reminder of why I was out in Malta, fighting to keep my family and others just like them safe from Hitler's savage ways. And perhaps she had brought me a little luck as well. I had survived lots of air raids, dog-fights and even the Wellington being hit. There were plenty who hadn't.

'Here we are,' said the nurse, returning a couple of hours later with a metal mug of thin broth.

'Did you find my jacket?' I asked, realising that I must sound a little deranged focussing on something so seemingly unimportant.

'I'm afraid it's a bit torn and very muddy. But I did find it. I'll bring it to you as soon as I can.'

She helped sit me up just enough so that I could sip the tasteless broth but my chest hurt too much. I set the mug down and shuffled my heavy leg, clad in a plaster cast, down the bed so I could lie flat again.

It was another three or four hours before the nurse finally came back with my jacket.

'I'm sorry,' she said. 'It's been another busy day I'm afraid. I've just finished my shift so I thought I'd drop this round for you before I go back to quarters.'

'Thank you,' I said. 'Very much.'

I managed to put my hand in the pocket as she held it out to me and felt an enormous sense of relief as I pulled out Susan Rabbit, along with the photo of my family.

'How darling,' the nurse said. 'Was she given to you by someone special?'

'My sister,' I told her. 'She made him for luck.'

'Well, it certainly seems to have worked. Now I'm going to get some sleep and I suggest you try and do the same.'

* * *

I had plenty of time to think in my hospital bed with nothing to do except listen to the screams and cries of some of the other patients and to wait for the nurses to come and take my temperature or pulse now and again.

For four days I just lay there thinking about Bill, Sheepy and all the other friends I'd lost. It was a difficult time and my mind went to some very dark places. I cried quietly at night when nobody could see me. I ached physically but the mental pain was a thousand times worse. The sheer ridiculousness of what we were all doing made me frustrated and angry.

'John,' said a familiar and very welcome voice on my fifth day in hospital.

'Jellicoe!' I said. 'I tried to find out if you'd survived but nobody could tell me. It's so good to see you.'

'I would have come to see you sooner, but this is the first chance I've had.'

'You obviously did a better job of landing than I did,' I laughed.

'Was there ever any doubt in that?' It was Jellicoe's turn to laugh.

'What about McHugh and Albright?'

'Both safe. Sheepy saved us all.'

There was no need to say anything else. We both knew that we'd never forget Elmer Mutton or the great courage he'd shown.

'Hey, darky,' snarled a man four beds away from mine. 'This ain't no place for people like you.'

Jellicoe and I pretended we hadn't heard the toxic man. We chatted on together but the man obviously had a point he was keen to make.

'Didn't you hear me? This is a place of rest for heroes. We can't be expected to convalesce if we're having to watch our backs with your kind around.'

I couldn't stay quiet any longer, despite Jellicoe laying his hand on my arm to stop me.

'If this is a place for heroes then my friend is precisely where he should be,' I shouted angrily. 'Maybe more so than you.'

'How dare you!' the man said. His face was an ugly twist of hatred and anger.

'Leave it,' said Jellicoe.

'No,' I said. I didn't often choose confrontation but Jellicoe was one of the kindest and bravest men I'd ever met. I wasn't going to just lie there and let some fool think it was alright to treat him this way. I'd had a sharp lesson in the value of friendship with Bill and I would never again take a good friend for granted.

'It's true,' I said, trying to control my voice and not shout. 'You are here because your country is at war and we all had to sign up to do our duty. And how much did it cost you?'

'You're as bad as he is,' the angry man said.

'Nothing,' I went on. 'It cost you nothing. But Flight Sergeant Jellicoe Hyde chose to be here. He could be at home living with his family on the other side of the Atlantic, away from all this. But he chose to come and play his part in this war. And to do so he paid good money to make the dangerous ocean journey. His own money, his own choice and his own danger. In my books that makes him a hero of the very finest sort.'

The man's face had gone crimson whilst I had been talking.

'Someone, get him out of here,' he said, standing up and jabbing a crutch in Jellicoe's direction.

'Excuse me sir,' said the man in the bed next to mine. 'But you are not the reason I signed up to fight for my country.'

To begin with I thought he was joining in with the abuse but then I realised his irritation was aimed at the man waving his crutch.

'Nor I,' added a man on the other side of the ward. 'If this gentleman is fighting alongside us then he is one of us.'

'I'd better go,' said Jellicoe, looking very uneasy. 'See you when you get back to Luqa. Although if I were you, I'd stay here as long as they let you. What I'd do for a few nights in a clean bed with nurses bringing me food.' He grinned but I could tell that it was a mask to hide his humiliation.

As he walked past the man with the crutches, I thought I could see him lift his chin just a little higher.

'Good riddance,' yelled the man. I watched in horror as he threw his crutch at Jellicoe, catching him on the back of the knee, making his legs buckle. Jellicoe righted himself and stood tall then he stooped to retrieve the crutch and walked over to the man who'd thrown it.

'I do believe you lost this,' Jellicoe said. He passed it back, keeping steady eye contact with the man.

The man lunged forward to snatch the crutch but overbalanced and fell, hands flailing as he tried to catch hold of something. Jellicoe caught him in his strong arms and supported his weight as the man tried desperately to find his footing. Jellicoe managed to manoeuvre the struggling chap onto his bed and then, when he was safe, Jellicoe laid both crutches next to him.

'Take care,' Jellicoe said. 'And I wish you luck.'

'Well-handled sir,' said one of the other patients as Jellicoe walked past.

'Proud to have you with us,' said another.

I knew that there'd always be people like the crutch man, ready to hate for no reason other than difference. But it warmed my heart to see Jellicoe's dignified response and to see him being recognised for it.

CHAPTER 13

Every morning for the rest of that week, Eliza and Boo went to meet Jonno and Scout. They walked through the woods and talked and talked. He told her more about secondary school and what to expect. Somehow listening to him made it seem just a little bit less scary. Eliza was definitely not looking forward to going but at least she'd stopped feeling like she might be sick every time she thought about it.

'Do you know what the best thing is?' said Jonno.

'What?' asked Eliza.

'If you don't like the person you have to sit next to in maths, you get to leave them behind when you go to geography. And if you don't like the person you sit next to in geography then you leave them behind when you go to art.'

'What if I don't like the person I sit next to in art?' Eliza said.

'Then you're just far too fussy and they get to leave you behind when they go to P.E,' said Jonno.

'Oi!' Eliza said.

'I just mean that you get to change around with your lessons. And with that many people all flowing through your days, it's much easier to find the people you want to be friends with. And it's easier to lose the ones who make life difficult.'

Eliza thought about Amy and her little gang.

'Did any of those sorts of people ever bother you at school?' she asked.

'Look at me,' he said, holding his arms out, still covered in the same green jumper he'd been wearing all week. 'I dress in the height of fashion, I'm very good looking.'

Eliza snorted.

'*Very* good looking,' he repeated, glaring at her over his glasses. 'Not to mention hysterically funny and an all-round brilliant person. But yes, despite all of this, there were people who liked to pick on me. But I figured out if I ignored them, or worse still, if I was actually nice to them, they got bored and left me alone.'

Just like Jellicoe thought Eliza.

'Doing anything this weekend?' he asked as they got back to the park.

'I think Mum and I might be having the day together tomorrow,' said Eliza. 'But I don't know what we're doing.'

'Nice,' said Jonno.

'I can walk on Sunday if you're not busy though.'

'Sunday it is,' said Jonno. 'Have a great day with your mum tomorrow. And don't forget to make her take your dad out on a date so Ganny can babysit you.'

'Not that I need babysitting,' Eliza said.

'No, it's just all for the cause,' agreed Jonno.

'You could come over if you like,' said Eliza. She'd been

wanting to ask him for days but the shy part of her had still had to build up the confidence.

'Yeah,' said Jonno. 'Not Sunday though as Grandma always makes us roast. Maybe Monday though?'

'Great,' said Eliza. 'You can meet Ganny.'

'Cool.'

'Though I should warn you that there's something a bit...' Eliza stopped, trying to think how to explain about Ganny's habit of talking to an empty chair.

'A bit what?' Jonno asked. 'Whatever it is, it can't be that bad. All families have their things. If I told you all of mine, we'd be here all week.'

Eliza took a deep breath.

'Do you believe in ghosts?' she asked.

'Not what I was expecting,' Jonno grinned. 'Why did you ask?'

'My Ganny believes,' Eliza said. 'She thinks her brother comes to visit, even though he died almost eighty years ago. It's rubbish of course but I wanted to warn you, just in case she says something and, you know...'

Jonno looked surprisingly thoughtful for a moment as though he was thinking very carefully about what to say next.

'Keep an open mind,' he said. 'And don't worry about me.'

* * *

As soon as she let Boo off the lead when they got back home, he trotted happily into the sitting room and flopped down next to the empty chair. Eliza waited by the door for a bit.

'Looks like you've made a friend there, John,' she heard Ganny say. 'You always did have a way with dogs. Do you remember old Suzie. She was such a sweet thing wasn't she. I don't think I ever heard her growl, not even once.'

There was a pause and then Ganny continued.

'Yes, well that was your own fault. I think I'd snap a little too if someone with feet as big as yours stood on my tail.'

Eliza coughed as she walked into the sitting room.

'Ah there you are, Darling,' said Ganny. 'Did you and Boo have a lovely walk with Jonno?'

'Yes thanks,' said Eliza. 'The house smells amazing.'

'There's a ginger cake in the oven, as you requested,' said Ganny. 'It'll be done in about ten minutes.'

Eliza smiled. Ganny's ginger cake was Dad's favourite and this was bound to make him think again about sending her to the home. Lose Ganny and he'd lose freshly baked ginger cake. It's not as though Mum was about to pick up her cooking apron and start baking teatime treats these days.

'Is it pushy of me to stick my nose in and say how wonderful it is to see you looking so happy this week?' Ganny asked.

'No,' said Eliza. 'I think I am happier.'

'That's good news,' said Ganny. 'Very good. Now I'm not one to play debt collector but this week I have mended three of your socks, fixed your school bag and baked a ginger cake at your request.'

Eliza nodded. 'All true,' she said.

'Which means I believe I am owed…'

'Char and chat time,' finished Eliza.

'Exactly.'

'I'll go and put the kettle on,' said Eliza.

Whilst Eliza brewed Ganny's Earl Grey tea in her favourite teapot, Ganny opened the oven door to check the cake.

'That's not what I think it is, is it?' Dad said, coming into the kitchen and breathing in deeply.

'Ganny's baked her prize-deserving ginger cake if that's what you mean,' said Eliza.

'It's not ready quite yet,' said Ganny. 'Why don't you sit down with us for ten minutes and have a cuppa until it's ready.'

Dad looked at the door, then he took out his phone and checked the screen.

'Go on then,' he said. 'Ten minutes can't hurt.'

Eliza got out an extra mug and threw a teabag into it. Dad wasn't one for fancy tea, he preferred it dark and milky with the bag left in.

'This is nice,' said Mum.

'Hello love,' said Dad, giving her a kiss. 'I thought you wouldn't be back until late today.'

'My last meeting was cancelled and it was much closer to come straight home than back to the office so I thought I'd work from here this afternoon.'

She hung her keys on the peg and kicked off her high heels.

'Is that Ganny's ginger cake I smell?' she asked.

'You're just in time for a slice,' said Eliza. 'Fresh from the oven.'

Ganny took the cake out and turned it upside down over the cooling rack. Sweet-smelling steam filled the kitchen and Eliza's stomach gurgled. She took out four plates and four forks. When was the last time they'd all shared a cup of tea and a slice of cake as a family in the middle of a Friday afternoon? She couldn't remember.

'Cup of tea?' she asked Mum.

'Ooh yes please love,' said Mum.

Tea made and cake cut, Eliza went to sit down at the table next to Ganny who was already in her favourite seat.

'Aren't you coming?' she asked Dad who was gobbling his cake whilst still standing in the kitchen.

'Sorry Fizzy Lizzy,' he said. 'I've got a call in a minute.'

'Mum?' Eliza said.

'I'll take mine in the office,' she said. 'I've got masses to get through this afternoon.'

'But your meeting was cancelled,' said Eliza, feeling the family bubble of happiness burst.

'And I'm grateful it was,' said Mum. 'Gives me the chance to catch up with everything else.'

'But we can still do something nice together tomorrow can't we?' said Eliza.

'We'll see,' said Mum. 'It depends how well I get on this afternoon.'

Eliza knew only too well what that meant. Work first, family second. She should have arranged to meet up with Jonno after all.

'Mum, ' she called as Mum's back disappeared through the kitchen door.

'What is it, Eliza?' Mum asked. 'Can it wait?'

'I was just going to tell you that you've got a hole in your cardigan. Maybe Ganny could stitch it up for you.'

CHAPTER 14

MALTA - NOVEMBER 1941 TO FEBRUARY 1942

There was absolutely no way I was going to be able to get passage back to England but I had another place to go when I was released from hospital.

Azalea and Maurice had been to see me and had offered a spare bed at the farm until I was ready to return to Luqa.

'You sleep here,' Azalea said.

I was touched to see a corner of their living space had been set up with a camp bed, a fresh sheet and blankets. There was a little table next to it with a small vase of fresh flowers that she must have picked for me.

'You are both so kind,' I said. 'You remind me of my sister, Liffy.'

Azalea smiled and said something to Maurice in Maltese. He smiled too and ushered me to a chair where I gratefully sat and set my crutches to one side.

Maurice had a ruddy face that looked as though it had seen many years of work outside on the farm. His eyes still sparkled despite the desperate hardships he must have seen. We were separated by a language barrier but that didn't stop us forming a quiet friendship. As the days rolled on, the three of us would sit together in the evenings and I quickly grew to adore their companionship. It was the closest thing to a family life I had been part of since the last time I'd seen my own family.

Although I'd been away from home for less than a year, I felt at least ten years older.

According to the Times of Malta, November saw the 1000th air raid on the island. And there was no sign of things easing.

'I've been called back,' I told Azalea, two weeks after my release from hospital.

'No,' she said. 'You not well. Leg not good. How can you fly?'

'I won't be,' I said. 'At least not until the plaster comes off and I'm fit for purpose. No, they need me in Valletta. They're short of radio operators and that's something I can do with my leg in plaster.'

'Missier[5] will be sad to say goodbye.'

'I'll miss him too. And you of course. It's been wonderful staying with you both and I can't thank you enough for your wonderful hospitality. I'll come and visit,' I promised. 'As often as I can. And I'll help on the farm when my leg is better.'

The day I left, Azalea and Maurice waved me off, arm

---

5   Grandfather

in arm in front of the farmhouse that had been my home for a short time.

* * *

I wasn't sent back to Luqa as I needed to stay in Valletta to be near the war rooms of Lascaris where I was to work as a wireless operator under the command of Wing Commander Barnum.

A girl called Sarah showed me the ropes on my first day.

'Not very glamorous I'm afraid,' she said as we left the green of the public gardens behind us and entered 'The Hole' as Sarah called it.

'Not much glamour left anywhere on Malta these days,' I said.

'Oi, cheeky,' Sarah said, tossing her hair.

'Oh. No,' I flushed. 'I didn't mean...'

'I'm just messing with you,' Sarah giggled. 'Come on, this way.'

'Miss Eversham,' the guard nodded to Sarah before turning to me. 'Pass please sir.'

I showed him the official pass I'd been given that allowed me to enter and we descended into the bomb proof tunnels cut deep into the limestone below.

The underground war rooms of Lascaris reminded me of an ants' colony with lots of tunnels full of people rushing about. There were different rooms for different jobs. I, of course, was located with RAF Fighter Control.

'I've been told to take you straight to Wing Commander Barnum,' Sarah said. 'He's in the RAF Operations Room.'

We walked into a room with a huge map of Malta, Sicily and the surrounding sea on a board. Charts were stuck to the walls and in the middle of the room was a vast table marked into squares. Surrounding the table were a group of people wearing headphones, pushing pieces across the table using long sticks.

'Those are the plotters,' Sarah said. 'They keep us up to date with what's going on out there.'

'Ah, Miss Eversham,' said a man with a booming voice. 'This must be Flight Sergeant Hallett?'

He held out his hand and I shook it. 'How's the old leg?' asked Wing Commander Barnum.

'Improving, I think, Sir,' I said. 'We'll find out in a few weeks when this blasted cast finally comes off. I hope to be back in the sky before too long.'

'Very good. Well, we can certainly put you to good use here in the meantime.'

* * *

I didn't mind my time at Lascaris. I was in as safe a place as any on Malta and that offered me a little respite of sorts. My job was to keep in contact with our planes as they flew into battle or on important missions. I relayed the information to the plotters. But more importantly, we also received news from the radar and observation stations as to the whereabouts of enemy planes. I was then able to keep our planes in the skies up to date with who they might suddenly find themselves up against.

It was fascinating work and vital to the running of the RAF but I longed to be back in Luqa with Jellicoe, Albie and the rest of the chaps. I felt as though that was where I belonged.

'You can almost plan your day by the raids,' Sarah said to me one day and she was right. At that time we were being bombed every morning, often at lunch time and then again in the early evening. Our boys were being kept on their toes and I was desperate to re-join them.

My plaster cast came off at the beginning of December. But my leg was still weak, as were my lungs, so I remained at Valletta and continued to spend my days operating the radios at Lascaris. I was frustrated but the doctor warned me that if I returned to the air too soon, the damage to my lungs could be very problematic with the change of pressure. I tried to argue but I was misunderstood and sent to the RAF rest camp in the north of the island for a few days. Even in December the water at St Paul's Bay was warmer than any British sea I'd ever set foot in. Swimming in the blue was unutterably glorious, but I couldn't enjoy it any more than I could 'rest' at the rest camp knowing what was happening to the island.

I did enjoy visiting Azalea and Maurice as often as possible from Valletta. I made sure to go round on Christmas Day. My first away from England and away from my family.

'I wish I could have brought you gifts,' I said when Azalea opened the door.

'It is good to see you,' she grinned. 'Come inside.'

'I did bring you biscuits,' I said, offering a packet I'd managed to barter for at the hotel I was staying at in Valletta.

'Grazzi, grazzi!'[6] Maurice said, as though I were

---

6   Thank you.

Scrooge at the end of A Christmas Carol, sending an entire feast around to the Cratchett family rather than just a tiny packet of plain biscuits.

'What is Christmas in England?' Azalea asked.

I didn't need long to think about that.

'It is wonderful,' I answered. 'Always cold. Sometimes we even have snow. Liffy loves the snow. She's always the first person out with her warmest clothes on.'

'I would like Liffy I think,' Azalea said.

'You would,' I agreed. 'And she would love you. Christmas is her favourite time of the year. She starts preparing for it as soon as December is here. Her bedroom is always covered in coloured streamers and she writes so many cards. There's one for everybody she knows, even the shop keepers and the postman.'

Thinking about Liffy at Christmas made me desperate to be there with her and my parents. Last year, rationing had meant a smaller feast than usual but we'd still sat around the table together to eat before playing games and listening to the wireless. I'd been restless and distracted, a boy ready to join up. How different things were just twelve months later.

We talked about our own Christmas traditions. Azalea's Christmases had started at church with a brass band playing and the community rejoicing.

'We come back here and eat good food and drink good wine,' she told me. 'My family together and happy. We sing and we dance. Then we go to see friends and have more good food.'

She looked sadly around the bare room and I knew she was thinking how different things had become for her too. We must all have had the same wishes and hopes at the front of our minds as we shared what Christmas cheer we could.

* * *

Finally, in January of 1942 I was called back to Luqa. So many crew members had been lost and those of us still standing were very much needed, gammy leg and chest or not.

'How are you feeling?' Jellicoe asked, the first time I took my goggles and helmet from the crew room and prepared for flight.

'A bit wobbly,' I replied. 'If I'm completely honest.'

'I understand that,' said Jellicoe. 'I felt the same the first time I kitted up after we went down.'

'What if I panic and I don't remember what to do?'

Jellicoe took me by the shoulders and looked me straight in the eyes.

'You will,' he said. 'You will remember because you have to.'

And of course I did remember. My chest ached with the change of pressure as we took to the sky. But I quickly got used to it.

Flying and fighting and watching and operating the radio, there was no time to worry about aches, feel any fear or think about anything at all other than the job at hand.

January marked the anniversary of the day I signed up to join the RAF and the day I last saw Bill. January also saw my grand promotion to Warrant Officer. I was proud of course and I knew if I could get word back to my family they'd be even prouder, especially Liffy.

'Congratulations,' said Jellicoe. 'Well earned.'

'It should have been you really,' I said. 'You're the better airman and a top rate navigator.'

'Not to mention a superior parachutist!' he teased.

'Ah yes,' I agreed. 'That goes without saying.'

Neither of us said it, but Jellicoe knew as well as I did that if he had been born in Surrey instead of Jamaica then it almost certainly would have been him receiving the promotion.

CHAPTER 15

Eliza was disappointed but not really surprised when Saturday came and Mum was too busy to take her out in the morning and too tired in the afternoon.

On Sunday, she made Ganny her morning cup of Earl Grey and took it into her room.

'You are such a good girl,' Ganny said.

She flicked the duvet back and Eliza snuggled in beside her.

'Open that top drawer, Darling,' said Ganny.

Eliza leant over and opened the drawer of Ganny's bedside table. On top of a pile of lacy hankies was an open packet of chocolate digestives. Eliza took them out.

'These?' she asked.

'That's it,' said Ganny. 'I sometimes buy a pack and hide them away. When I was a child I thought having biscuits by my bed to wake up to was the very best idea, but I was never allowed. Then I grew up and I was allowed but I realised it was not really the done thing. But now I've grown up even more and I find I don't always care for the done thing.'

Ganny opened the packet and offered it to Eliza. She took one and had to agree with Ganny that it really was the very best idea. The two of them sat in Ganny's bed watching cartoons and nibbling chocolate biscuits.

'What my mother would say if she could see us,' Ganny giggled. 'I feel like a naughty imp.'

'Did you and John get up to mischief when you were little,' asked Eliza, picking crumbs from the duvet cover.

'Oh, all the time,' Ganny chuckled. 'He was a real trickster and he always roped me in too. I think that was so whenever we were discovered, he could try and pin the blame on me.'

'What did you do?' Eliza asked.

'A lot of our trickery was with one thing in mind,' began Ganny. 'Biscuits.'

'Biscuits?'

'Yes. Biscuits. Or chocolate, cake, sticky buns, anything sweet really. You see we both had a very sweet tooth. If we ever had any money we'd go to the village shop and buy twists of pear drops or sherbet. But we had to hide them from Mum or else she would have confiscated them straight away. Daddy was allowed biscuits though. He kept an old tartan tin in his study, next to the fireplace and it was always full of shortbread or gypsy creams. And every Saturday he would visit the chocolate shop and choose a quarter for Mum to have as a treat after she'd cooked our Sunday roast. '

'But nothing for you and Uncle John?'

'I'm not being completely fair,' Ganny admitted. 'Clara, our home help, baked a treat once a week and we had a little money every Saturday for sweets. But they had to last us all week and we had usually finished them within ten minutes of getting them home. And we always craved more so we spent far too much time thinking up ways to snaffle a chocolate from Mummy's bag or a biscuit from Daddy's tin.'

'What did you do?' Eliza asked.

'We always worked as a pair,' said Ganny. 'Usually John caused a distraction, pretending to fall down the stairs, shouting blue murder from his bedroom, knocking on the door and then running away, that sort of thing. And then I'd creep up to the treats and steal one for each of us. I never took too much because greed was a sure way of being found out. But for me the treat was only a very tiny part of the enjoyment. Far better than the chocolate itself was the joy of teaming up with John and then hiding in the big coat cupboard with him, nibbling the spoils of our trickery and giggling away together when we thought of how cunning we'd been.'

Eliza thought for the millionth time how much she wished she wasn't an only child. But then Ganny had been made one too by the time she was sixteen and John had left for Malta.

'Ganny,' she said. 'How did you really find out about John's time in Malta? Did he leave a diary or letters that you used to write his story?'

Ganny sighed.

'You will believe what you're ready to believe,' she said.

'What does that mean?' Eliza asked.

'It means that we've been lying in bed for too long and the day is marching away from us.'

* * *

Eliza had been looking forward to Jonno's visit all weekend, but when Monday arrived, she suddenly felt nervous about the whole thing. What if he didn't like the house? Or even worse, what if he didn't like Ganny? What if Ganny started talking to the empty chair and Jonno thought she was barmy, despite what he'd said to her in the wood.

She stopped worrying as soon as he arrived and she saw him and Scout walking up the path to the front door. He stopped and ran his fingers through his hair and Eliza wondered if he was ever going to ring the doorbell. Maybe he was nervous too. She opened the door and Scout ran straight in and did a little dance in the hallway with Boo before the pair of them pelted out of the open back door and did a few laps of the garden at top speed. By the time Eliza had shown Jonno into the kitchen, the dogs had settled into sniffing every inch of the garden, side by side.

'Do you want a drink?' Eliza asked. 'I'm making tea for Ganny or you could have juice or chocolate milk?'

'I'm fine thanks,' said Jonno.

Dad walked in then, looking harassed and busy.

'Have you seen my portable charger?' he said.

'No, sorry,' said Eliza. 'Dad, this is Jonno. I told you he was coming round today.'

Dad looked up with a frown on his face.

'What?' he said crossly. 'Eliza, I've no time for this right now. I need that charger. If you find it could you bring it into the office please.'

He stalked from the kitchen without even saying hello to Jonno. Eliza's cheeks pinked in embarrassment.

'I'm really sorry,' she said. 'He's not usually quite that rude. He must be having a difficult day.'

'It's fine,' said Jonno.

'Are you sure you don't want a drink?'

Jonno shook his head. 'I like your house,' he said. 'The garden's really cool. You've even got a pond.'

He walked over to the door and looked outside to where Ganny was sitting under a sunshade with a blanket tucked across her knees.

'You must be Jonno,' Ganny said. 'Eliza has told me all about you.'

'Ganny!' said Eliza.

'She's told me all about you as well,' said Jonno. 'But I don't know what to call you. I only know you as Ganny.'

'That will do just perfectly,' Ganny smiled. 'Have you two got important business or have you time to come and sit in the sun for a little while. I've been watching the dragon flies over the pond. They remind me of little fighter planes, nipping about and dodging each other.'

Eliza put a tray on the table and handed Ganny her mug of Earl Grey. She passed the biscuit tin to Ganny who took two and laid them on her knee.

'Jonno?' Eliza asked, passing the tin to him.

'No thanks,' said Jonno. 'I'm alright.'

'Really?' said Eliza.

'Not everyone shares our appetite for biscuits, Darling,' said Ganny. 'Isn't that right, Jonno?'

'Do you want to sit out here or do something else?' Eliza asked, suddenly feeling awkward again.

'Here's good,' Jonno said.

Taking a seat, he turned to Ganny.

'Eliza told me about the book you wrote,' he said. 'The one about your brother.'

'I'm delighted she's reading it,' said Ganny. 'She can hold John's story long after I've gone. And maybe pass it on to her own children one day.'

'Best way of keeping stories alive,' said Jonno. 'I loved hearing my Gramps tell me about his memories. He was born after the war though. A shocker of a teenager in the sixties I think.'

'Lots were,' said Ganny. 'My daughter Penny being one of them.'

'I miss him,' said Jonno.

'When did he die?' Eliza asked.

'Oh, he hasn't,' said Jonno. 'We just can't see each other anymore.'

Jonno didn't give any more detail and neither Eliza nor Ganny asked. Somehow it just didn't seem right.

'You learnt some cool stuff from your Dad,' said Jonno. 'Eliza told me he taught you how to put out fires and even how to drive a truck.'

'Not a truck,' said Ganny. 'Just our old Austin Seven. But I could get her to fly round corners pretty fast.'

'I'd love to learn to drive,' said Jonno.

Ganny clearly enjoyed having someone new to tell her stories to and Jonno seemed to be really interested. The three of them talked for ages about the Home Guard and Ganny's life. Then she talked a bit about John and his time in Malta. Eliza was sent inside to fetch some of Ganny's old photos and John's flying cap and medals. When she got back she could see Ganny talking to an empty chair.

Oh no, Eliza thought. *Jonno will think she's round the bend.* She was glad she'd warned him about Ganny's ghost habit. But then Jonno looked at the empty chair and he started talking to it too.

'Eliza's thinks I'm going loopy,' Ganny said when Eliza

stepped out into the garden. 'Talking to my long dead brother.'

'And I've told Eliza she should keep an open mind,' said Jonno with a grin.

CHAPTER 16

MALTA - MARCH 1942

Life in Malta was pretty grim as 1942 progressed. Supply ships were key targets and any that tried to navigate the Mediterranean to bring us food, medical supplies and vital fuel were heavily bombed.

In March, a convoy of four ships were sent to our aid and miraculously three of them arrived in Grand Harbour. But unforgivably poor planning meant that the ships docked without proper resources to unload them and store the supplies. For two nights, they remained in dock. And then, on the third day, the whole lot were bombed and all supplies lost.

Even heavier rationing came in and Malta began to slowly starve.

I went to visit Azalea and Maurice at every opportunity. It wasn't as easy as when I'd been in Valletta, but I took a bicycle if there was one available or sometimes I managed to hitch a lift to the town and make the hour's walk from there to the farm.

One day, I met Azalea on the road just outside Valletta. She was heading in to buy what food she could manage with her coupons.

We walked together, chatting and even sharing a joke or two about a goat she remembered who had been on the farm when she was a young girl. She really had become like a sister to me and I enjoyed her company greatly.

'I go to the kitchen,' she said.

'I'll come with you,' I said. 'You can tell me more about your old goat whilst we queue.'

The Victory Kitchen in Valletta always had a long queue snaking away from it as people lined up to collect their allocated food.

'Bettina was trouble always,' Azalea giggled. 'All goats eat much. But Bettina ate much that was not food. My clean stockings one day, Ommi's good hat and the head of my doll.'

'Oh, my word,' I said in mock horror. 'Your poor doll. How sad to live without a head.'

'Ommi made a new head for her.'

She smiled. 'I still love her now.'

I took Susan Rabbit from my pocket and showed her to Azalea.

'Liffy made her for me. I think things made by people we love are far better.'

'She brings you luck I think,' said Azalea.

'Yes,' I said. 'I really believe she does.'

When we finally got to the front of the queue, Azalea passed over two little rationing slips and a few coins worth around six pence. For this she was given two slices of oddly black bread and six herrings in tomato sauce. That would have to keep her and Maurice going until the next day when she'd come back to the Victory Kitchen to collect her next rationed allowance of food.

'I show you my church,' she said as we walked away. 'It not far.'

The church was simple but beautiful. Made from the pale Maltese limestone with a tall bell tower. Inside it felt cool and peaceful. We both knelt at a pew and I muttered a prayer in the hope that it might help in some way. I wasn't Catholic like Azalea, but I thought it certainly couldn't do any harm.

'We must thank Santa Marija for keeping us safe,' Azalea said and she showed me a marble statue of Mary holding a tiny baby in her arms. She looked so tranquil and content and I prayed that one day all mothers would be able to look that way at their babies.

'I must go,' I said. 'I have to get back to Luqa but I'll come and see you again as soon as I can. I haven't got another day off for a while but please don't think I have forgotten you as the time passes.

We'd walked for fifteen minutes or so before we stopped at a junction where we needed to part company. Suddenly, as we were saying goodbye, the all too familiar noise of the air raid sirens broke the air around us.

'We go back to church,' Azalea said. 'There is safety underground there.'

I knew that many of the churches had crypts beneath them and that these were a popular place to shelter so I took Azalea's hand and we ran back in the direction of the church. We could hear a thrumming drone above us and I could tell without looking that the noise belonged to German planes.

'Come on,' I yelled.

We hurtled down the road but, before we reached the church, there was an almighty explosion ahead. The force lifted me clean off my feet and flung me several yards backwards where I landed with a crash. My ears were full of the ringing sounds the bomb had left behind and my eyes were stinging from great clouds of dust. I covered my mouth with my hand and scrabbled to my feet.

'Azalea,' I shouted. 'Azalea!'

I could see movement around me. First a man and his young son, then an old lady who I helped to her feet. But I couldn't see any sign of Azalea.

'Azalea,' I yelled again.

And then I saw her. Lying on top of a pile of rubble with blood dripping from a large cut on her forehead. For a terrible moment I thought she had been killed in the blast but, as I went to check her, I could see her chest rising and falling.

I stroked the dust clogged hair from her face and almost wept with relief when her eyes blinked open.

'Can you walk?' I asked.

With my help, she managed to get to her feet. The planes were still overhead and the sirens were still wailing so it wasn't safe to be out in the open.

'We need to get to the church,' I said. 'Can you manage it?'

'I think so,' she said.

Our progress was slow as the air was still dusty and the rubble beneath our feet made running impossible. The noise of the planes moved away but the sirens continued. My leg hurt and breathing was tricky again but we made our way as quickly as we could towards the refuge of the church and its crypt.

The wailing of the sirens stopped as we reached the square but it was replaced with a sound even worse. The wails and cries of humans,

'The church has been hit,' I said in utter horror.

'No!' Azalea exclaimed. 'Santa Marija!'

But there was no denying the horrific sight that met our eyes. The church we'd been standing in less than half an hour earlier, was now no more than a single wall, standing tall and lonely as a soldier in a field of fallen comrades. All around lay piles of stone that had been the rest of the building, covering the crypt we'd been heading for, like a heavy rock blanket smothering everything and everyone below.

'Ghajnuna!'[7] a man cried.

'They need help,' yelled Azalea. 'There are people under the church.'

'Shhhhh,' another man shouted. 'Isma!'[8]

'He's telling us to listen,' Azalea whispered.

A deathly hush fell on the square. We listened in the desperate hope that we might hear a sound indicating life beneath the rubble. But there was nothing.

'We should start digging,' I said after a few minutes.

I started shifting rocks and throwing them to the side

7   Help
8   Listen

but there was just so much and it felt like a fruitless task. Still, we had to try.

Everyone present did the same. Shifting the rubble and hoping to find some sign of life below. Every now and again we'd stop and listen but there was nothing. We dug anyway. My fingernails ripped and my hands became scratched and sore but we carried on.

'Shhh,' said Azalea suddenly. 'Shhh.'

We all stopped and kept still and silent as she pointed to a spot in the rubble. To begin with I heard nothing. And then a very tiny noise. A snuffling, whimpering, very human noise.

That was all we needed to hear. We focussed our efforts on that one spot, lifting and digging until we found something that warmed and froze my very core at the same time.

'Tarbija,'[9] Azalea said. 'It's a baby.'

The head of a small child could just be seen. She was covered by the body of a woman, her mother probably.

Between us we gently managed to move the woman out of the way and pull out the tiny, wriggling infant who looked no more than about two years old.

'They must have been on the steps going down into the crypt,' I said. 'Her mother's body cushioned her and saved her life.'

Azalea hugged the child tightly, cradling her head carefully. The little girl was wide eyed and completely silent in her shock.

'Ask if anyone knows who she is,' I said.

---

9 Baby

Azalea shouted something in Maltese and a woman stepped forward, tears cleaning little tracks through the dust layer on her face. She spoke to Azalea and then buried her face in her hands and started to sob. A man put his arm around her shoulder and led her away.

'Well?' I asked.

'Her name is Abigail,' she said. 'Now her mother is dead, she has no family.'

'What do we do?' I asked.

Azalea lifted her chin up high and wrapped her arms even more tightly around the little girl.

'I am her family now. We look after her.'

CHAPTER 17

Eliza and Jonno were sitting in the den in the woods. Scout and Boo had chased every squirrel and rabbit they could sniff out and both were lying in exhausted heaps on the old kitchen flooring.

'Have you read any more of John's story?' Jonno asked. 'Last time you told me he'd been sent back to the airfield and was going to be back up in the skies again.'

'It sounds like things got even harder on Malta after that,' said Eliza. 'And I think he missed Ganny loads, especially at Christmas. But he had Azalea and Maurice, you remember, the ones on the farm who looked after him when he got out of hospital.'

'Yeah,' said Jonno. 'They sound awesome.'

'I think they were. First they took John in and then a little girl called Abigail who'd lost all of her family in the raids.'

Eliza told Jonno about everything she'd read. The air raid and the church that collapsed, trapping so many people in the crypt below.

'Whoa,' said Jonno when she got to the bit about how they'd pulled Abigail from the rubble. 'That poor little girl.'

They sat for a while and Eliza tried to imagine being in Valletta when the bombs fell. It must have been terrifying.

'Thanks for having me round yesterday,' said Jonno, breaking into her thoughts. 'I had a really good time. Your Ganny's really cool.'

'Thanks,' Eliza said. 'I'm glad I warned you about her and the whole ghost thing though so it wasn't too much of a weird shock when she started talking to an empty chair. Thanks for joining in with her too.'

'You should listen to her,' Jonno said. 'She seemed really sure about what she was seeing.'

Sharp as a pin and bright as a button, Eliza thought.

'Ghosts though,' Eliza said. 'Everyone knows they're not real.'

'Why?' Jonno said. 'Just because you haven't seen one.'

'I guess,' said Eliza. 'I wonder if there's a test or something we could do.'

'Or maybe you could just let her talk to her brother if it makes her happy and stop worrying about whether his ghost is real or just real to her.'

Eliza thought about it. It was something she'd thought about a lot and she still didn't know the answer. Jonno was right, on one hand it did make Ganny so happy. But on the other hand, it also made her look like she was losing her mind a bit and perhaps should be sent to a care home. She sighed.

'Now, more importantly, how is Operation Ganny going?' Jonno said.

'Could be better,' said Eliza dismally. 'She's cooked

all Mum and Dad's favourite things, mended loads of *accidentally* ripped clothes and she even put a new plug on the kettle, something her dad taught her to do.'

'How did you sort that one out?'

'That one wasn't actually me. The kettle broke on its own and Dad was going to throw it out but I remembered Ganny telling me how her dad always wanted to make sure she knew how to look after herself and that included wiring a plug.'

'Sounds like she's making herself very valuable indeed.'

'I thought so too,' said Eliza. 'But last night I asked Dad about it. Pointed out all the things she's done and all the ways she helps every day.'

'What did he say?'

'He said it was all very well but wiring a plug and baking ginger cake didn't make her legs any steadier and they were still worried she would have a fall,' said Eliza. 'Which is so stupid. She hasn't fallen for weeks now and her walking sticks help her when she's up and about.'

Jonno rubbed his chin. 'We need a bigger plan,' he said.

They sat and thought about it for a while but neither came up with anything particularly useful before it was time to head back to their homes for lunch.

* * *

After lunch, Eliza suggested a game of cards.

'Do you think you might wander up to the shops with me first?' Ganny asked. 'I don't like going on my own any more as my legs are wobblier than they used to be. I would love your arm to borrow, if you don't mind.'

Eliza was more than happy to help out. She fetched

Ganny's outdoor shoes and her handbag and watched as she stopped by the mirror in the hall to comb her hair and put on her bright pink lipstick.

'Right,' said Ganny. 'Ready.'

Eliza held out her elbow for Ganny to slip her skinny hand through. They walked slowly up the road into town and popped into the chemist for Ganny to collect her medicines. Then they went into the newsagent for a newspaper, a 90th birthday card for one of Ganny's friends back where she used to live, and a little white packet of her favourite boiled sweets that smelled of herbs and spices.

'I think I'll take a lottery card too,' Ganny said to the man behind the counter. 'I'm feeling lucky.'

'I'm afraid you need to be at least sixteen to buy a scratch card, young lady,' the man said. 'I'm going to have to see some proof of age.'

'You cheeky thing,' said Ganny, her eyes twinkling.

The man chuckled and tore off a scratch card. 'There you go, Elizabeth. See you again soon I hope.'

'Thank you, Owen. Please give my best wishes to Trish.'

'How do you know his name?' Eliza asked when they stepped outside.

'I make a point of finding out the names of people I meet,' said Ganny. 'Now let's see if we've won ourselves a fortune shall we. I feel like cruising to South Africa to ride on elephants and ostriches.'

She passed the card and a penny coin to Eliza who scratched off the little silver tabs.

'I think we've won,' Eliza said.

'Really?' Ganny said. 'Let me see.'

Eliza passed the card over.

'Well, I never,' said Ganny. 'We have won! A whole fifteen pounds. Not quite enough for our trip to Africa but definitely enough for a sticky bun at the Bluebird Tearooms.'

* * *

By the time they'd finished their buns and wandered back to the house, the afternoon had almost gone. Dad's car wasn't on the drive which meant he was probably out meeting a client. Either that or down at the gym trying to unwind.

Eliza opened the door and put Ganny's shopping bag on the bench.

'That was lovely, Darling,' said Ganny. 'Let's have another go soon. Maybe next time we'll hit the jackpot.'

'I hope so,' said Eliza. 'I quite like the idea of riding an elephant.'

'I think I shall prefer the ostriches,' said Ganny. 'And I'm pretty sure I could beat you in an ostrich race.'

Eliza could hear Mum on the phone in the kitchen. She and Ganny were just by the kitchen door when the ear-splitting sound of the fire alarms going off made Eliza jump out of her skin.

'Oh Lord,' said Mum, dropping her phone on the counter. 'I forgot about the oil!'

'Mum,' Eliza shouted. 'It's on fire!'

Behind Mum, a saucepan on the hob had tall orange flames dancing from it.

'Get out of there,' Ganny shouted.

But Mum didn't listen. She took a big jug from the windowsill and pulled out the flowers that were in it, chucking them on the floor.

'NO!' Ganny screamed.

But it was too late. Mum threw the jug of flower water onto the pan of burning oil and the whole thing exploded in a fire ball that caught Mum's floppy sleeve, setting it alight.

CHAPTER 18

MALTA - APRIL 1942

Life continued to be terribly hard in Malta but we did find reasons to lift our spirits. The first Spitfire planes arrived in Malta on March 11th to much excitement. They also brought new pilots which boosted our hopes in the skies.

The Hurricanes our boys had been flying had done us proud in the dog fights but they were old and patched up and fighter planes had moved on a lot since they'd been the cutting edge of the RAF. The Spitfires were a far better match for the Luftwaffe and the pilots were less jaded than those who had been out on Malta for so many months.

And then, in the Times of Malta on 17th April came news that boosted us all.

'Here,' said Albie at breakfast that day. 'Have you seen this?'

He thrust the paper onto the table and sat down next to me to drink his tea and eat his porridge.

There on the front page was a picture of King George VI beneath the headline;

THE KING AWARDS GEORGE CROSS TO MALTA

'What does it mean?' I asked. 'A medal can't be awarded to an entire island, can it?'

'Read on old chap,' said Albie.

'To honour her brave people,' I read, 'I award the George Cross to the Island Fortress of Malta to bear witness to a heroism and devotion that will long be famous in history.'

'Well, I never,' said Jellicoe. 'That can't happen very often.'

'No, I can't say it does,' Albie agreed.

'It does make it feel as though we are less alone out here, now that the King has recognised our little island.'

'Our island?' Albie said. 'I thought Blighty was our island.'

'I don't know,' I said. 'It feels as though we've been here long enough to call this place a home of sorts.'

'I think you're right my friend,' said Jellicoe. 'Home can be wherever you lay your hat.'

'And for now at least, that happens to be the most bombed place on the planet,' I said.

* * *

The new influx of pilots and their Spitfires meant that I was granted an unexpected full three days leave at the beginning of May. I went to the farm and spent my time off with Azalea, Maurice and little Abigail.

'She seems to have settled in with you,' I said.

'She is a very good child,' Azalea said proudly. 'Abigail, this is Mr John.'

She repeated it in Maltese and Abigail looked up shyly from Azalea's arms.

'Bongu Abigail,'[10] I said. 'Hello.'

The child buried her head once more into Azalea's chest. Azalea stroked her soft head and murmured softly into her ear.

'Maurice loves her,' Azalea said. 'She came from such sadness, is it right that she brings us much joy?'

'Anything that can bring joy to this war is definitely right,' I said. 'She might not have the family she was born to but she is loved and, with luck, she'll grow up to be happy.'

I spent such a happy time on the farm. It was almost as though the bombers knew we all needed the time to breathe and enjoy our small, thrown together family. We could hear the bombs fall in Valletta but the farm itself was untouched during that time.

I helped sowing new crops and milking the two cows that still remained on the farm. Every day I went into Valletta with Azalea to collect our daily rations. Abigail always stayed on the farm with Maurice. Partly because she was safer there and partly, I think, because Azalea didn't want her anywhere near the site of her tragedy.

The day before I was due to return to Luqa, Azalea and I were out in the chicken coop, collecting eggs.

'Not many to find,' Azalea said as we searched through the old hay. 'We eat most chickens long ago. And these ones are hungry just like us.'

---

10 Hello

We only found one egg that day. But it was one more than the previous day so that was cause for celebration. I knew without asking that the entire thing would be cooked up for Abigail.

'Malta is famous now,' I said. 'The Island of the George Cross.'

'It gives us hope,' said Azalea.

'It shows how much the King understands about the wonderful people of your island. You must hate us for bringing the war to you.'

'The war would come,' she said. 'You or the Germans would come. And if Hitler came to Malta.'

She shivered.

'I suppose so,' I said.

'Come,' she said. We shut the little wooden door of the chicken coop and leant on the fence, watching the scrawny few remaining birds scratch in the dirt for a bit. For a few precious moments the world seemed to be smiling. The spring Mediterranean sun was hot on our backs and the skin on my bare forearms. I forgot I was miles from home, hungry and living life with the constant threat that each day could be my last.

'Zaylee,' called a tiny voice. We turned to see Maurice and Abigail coming to find us. 'Zaylee,' the little girl called again as she struggled from Maurice's arms and ran across the farm to hug Azalea – or Zaylee as she had clearly renamed her.

'She is clever,' Azalea said.

'Of course she is,' I replied.

'I worry for her,' she said. 'I can't feed her enough and she needs to grow.'

'She looks as though she's doing brilliantly,' I tried to reassure her. 'And at least you have the well so you can keep her clean and let her drink. Most places have such a shortage of water that we can't flush the toilets or wash our hands too often. Can you imagine that at the base with all those filthy men.'

'Smells bad,' Azalea laughed pinching her nose.

'Smells very bad,' I said pinching mine too.

'Bah,' added Abigail and then she pinched her own nose making everybody giggle.

CHAPTER 19

Eliza screamed as panic set in. The back of the kitchen was being licked by the fire and Mum was fighting to bash out the flames on her arm. She turned on the tap and howled as she stuck her arm under the water

'Get out of there,' Ganny shouted. 'Come NOW.'

Mum was no longer alight herself but the fire was spreading fast. Hot oil had been thrown across the counter which was blazing in front of her. Mum was staring at the flames around her as though they'd somehow turned her into a statue. There was only a small gap for Mum to get past the counter so she could reach the door and the flames were quickly making that gap ever smaller.

'I can't do it,' said Mum.

'My blanket is out by the pond. Throw it in and get it wet and then bring it here as fast as you possibly can,' said Ganny.

Eliza was out of the door and back in a flash, the soaked blanket in her hands.

'Pass it to me,' said Ganny. 'Quick!'

Eliza watched as her great grandmother threw the blanket over herself like a tent and pushed her way through the flames into the burning kitchen. She reached Mum and held the blanket up so Mum could huddle under it with her. Eliza stared in horror as the flames licked the edges of the blanket and caught the bottom of Mum's baggy work trousers.

'Hurry up,' Eliza screamed.

Ganny and Mum emerged from the now fully burning kitchen and Ganny pushed the door shut behind them.

'Your leg,' Eliza screamed.

'Drop to the floor,' Ganny said. 'Roll around as much as you can.'

Mum threw herself onto the hall floor and rolled around until the flames that had been creeping up her trouser leg were out.

'Now get out,' Ganny said.

Mum was sobbing as Ganny and Eliza helped her out of the house and into the front garden with Boo whimpering at their feet.

'I know it hurts my darling,' Ganny said. 'But be brave. You'll be fine now.'

Mrs Cox from across the road came running over.

'I've called the fire brigade,' she said. 'They're on their way.'

'She's hurt,' Ganny said. 'Her arm and leg are burnt. Have you got some cling film?'

'Of course,' said Mrs Cox.

Mum half sat, half fell onto the bench outside Mrs Cox's house.

'You'll be okay Mum,' said Eliza. 'Ganny knows what to do.'

Mum squeezed Eliza's hand tightly and shut her eyes. Eliza tried not to look at the angry blistered skin on her other arm where the fire had started to eat her.

'Now my darling, I know this is so very sore,' Ganny said, sitting down on the bench next to Mum. 'But we need to protect that arm of yours until the ambulance gets here.'

Mrs Cox came out with a roll of cling film and passed it to Ganny.

'Could we have a bowl of water as well?' said Ganny calmly. 'Cold from the tap but not iced. And some cloths or towels.'

Ganny pulled a length of cling film from the roll and wrapped it around Mum's red and black arm. Mum gasped from the pain and gripped Eliza's hand even tighter.

'That's right my Poppet,' said Ganny. 'You brave girl. That's done.'

She looked at Eliza. 'I don't think I've got the energy to bend down and wrap her leg. Do you think you could do it?'

Eliza nodded and took the roll of film. She pulled out a long length and then started wrapping it around Mum's leg just as she had seen Ganny do. Luckily Mum's leg didn't look nearly as bad as her arm had. But Mum still twitched and gasped when the plastic touched the raw patches.

'Not too loose,' said Ganny. 'We need to keep the air away from it.

Wailing sirens and blue lights filled the street and two fire engines screeched up outside the house. The fire fighters jumped out and started pulling hoses from the back of the engine.

'Anyone in there?' shouted one of the fire fighters.

'No,' Ganny shouted back. 'We're all out.'

'Very good,' said the fire fighter and she ran back to join the rest of the team.

Ganny and Eliza used the towels to squeeze cool water over the film on Mum's burnt arm and leg, trying to take some of the heat out of it.

'I don't think she'd have coped with the pain if we had done this on her raw skin,' said Ganny.

Mum winced with pain but sat still and let them carry on.

Eliza watched what was happening around her as though it was a television show. Something happening to somebody else's family. The ambulance arrived and two friendly paramedics dressed in green overalls checked Mum over before helping her onto a stretcher and putting an oxygen mask over her face.

'Who used the cling film?' one of the paramedics said.

'It was Ganny,' said Eliza.

'With lots of help from you Poppet,' said Ganny.

'Well thank goodness you were here,' said the paramedic. 'You've certainly given her skin the very best chance of healing.'

Dad came running over.

'What happened?' he panted.

'Is this your family sir?' said the paramedic.

'Yes, that's my wife. Is she okay?'

'She's got some very nasty burns but this pair have been brilliant. Now we're going to give her a big old dose of pain killers to help her out and get her to the hospital.'

'Can I go with her?' asked Dad.

'Of course you can.'

'Will you be alright?' Dad said, looking at Eliza and Ganny.

'They can stay with me,' said Mrs Cox. 'Until we know what's what.'

'I just want to give them both a look over, check they didn't take in any smoke,' said the paramedic.

He listened to Ganny's chest and then Eliza's before asking them a few questions. Then he strapped them up to a machine that bleeped and showed a lot of numbers that Eliza didn't understand.

'All seems fine here. But I wouldn't mind taking you to hospital for a proper once over,' he said to Ganny. 'On account of your age.'

'I'm as strong as an ox,' Ganny told him. 'And I'm staying with my great grand-daughter.'

'Well, it is against my recommendation. But okay then, as long as you promise to call for help if you get at all tight-chested or experience anything else troubling.'

Ganny promised and Eliza watched the ambulance disappear down the road, taking Mum and Dad to the hospital.

'There's nothing more you can do here,' said Mrs Cox. 'Come on. We can sit and have a cup of tea whilst we wait for news.'

It was a little while before there was a knock on Mrs Cox's door and the fire fighter came in.

'You've been relatively lucky,' she said. 'The kitchen's a mess I'm afraid, but the rest of the house is fine. Whoever shut the door managed to stop it from spreading.'

'Can we go home now then?' Eliza asked.

'I'm afraid not. Whilst the rest of the house is structurally safe, the smoke damage will need to be dealt with by a fire restoration company before it's safe for you to move back in. Someone can go in and pack a few things to keep you going but they need to be as quick as possible and should cover their nose and mouth with a mask or scarf. Have you got somewhere you can stay?'

'They can all stay here with me,' said Mrs Cox.

'We couldn't possibly,' said Ganny.

'Rubbish,' said Mrs Cox. 'I have plenty of space now the children have gone. And it gets lonely on my own so I shall love having guests.'

'Boo as well?' Eliza asked.

'Definitely Boo as well.'

* * *

When Dad got back from the hospital it was getting pretty late.

'Is Mum going to be okay?' Eliza asked.

'She's very sore,' Dad said. 'And her arm might need a bit of extra attention once they see how well it's healing, but it looks as though she'll be absolutely fine. The doctor treating her said that you and Ganny did all the right things and she was lucky you were there.'

'We're always lucky to have Ganny with us,' said Eliza.

'I've got to go and fetch a few things from the house,' said Dad. 'Tell me what you need and I'll pick it up.'

'I'd like to come,' said Eliza.

'It won't be pretty,' Dad warned. 'And you'll have to be super quick.'

'That nice fire lady said you should cover your faces,' said Mrs Cox. 'Here take these.'

'Thank you,' said Eliza, taking one of the scarves Mrs Cox was holding out.

Eliza and Dad held hands as they crossed the street to their house.

'Scarf on,' said Dad. He helped her wrap it around her nose and mouth and then did the same with his own. It smelled of a musty old cupboard but it was better than the stink of burning that clogged the air outside the house.

Apart from the black doorway that led into the totally destroyed kitchen, everything else looked almost as it had done. The hallway was a mess. Mum would freak when she saw the muck and water all over the floor. But upstairs in her bedroom it was like nothing had changed to look at. Even through the scarf, the smell was another thing altogether. It was like the smell her coat and hair picked up when they went to watch the big bonfire being lit on Guy Fawkes' night, only a hundred times stronger.

'Be quick,' Dad called. 'Just take what you need for a night or two. We can always pop back if we need more.'

Eliza took her backpack from the bottom of the wardrobe and packed her pyjamas, spare clothes and soap bag. She took the journal and Alfie Bear and put them on top.

'Thank goodness you two are safe,' she said.

'Come on Fizzy Lizzy,' called Dad. 'The quicker we get out the better. I don't want you breathing in this air.'

As they were about to leave, Eliza darted back into the sitting room.

'Nothing else,' Dad said. 'Whatever it is can wait.'

'Just a second,' Eliza called. She went over to the table by Ganny's patch on the sofa and picked up the photo of John.

'You need to come with us,' she told him, before running out to meet Dad.

CHAPTER 20

MALTA - AUGUST 1942

By the summer, the island was on its knees and just weeks from surrender. We could hold out against the bombs and the enemy fire. But without food, the people of Malta were starving. And without fuel, our planes and submarines would be useless.

'This convoy is our last hope,' said Jellicoe one evening in August as we sat in the mess.

'Operation Pedestal they're calling it,' said Albie. 'Bringing food and fuel to rescue us all.'

'They're bringing more than that,' said Jellicoe. 'They're bringing hope and deliverance.'

We knew that a large number of ships had set off from Gibraltar heading our way with much needed essential supplies. But we also knew that Germany and Italy would be doing everything they could to make sure the ships didn't make it.

'At least this time we'll be ready for them when they do arrive,' said Albie. 'I was sent to Grand Harbour yesterday. They were putting up signs everywhere showing where everything is to go. And they've got the manpower to make sure it happens. None of this bombing in port nonsense like what happened in March.'

'Do you think they'll be bringing any decent bread, butter and jam?' I wondered. 'I never realised it would be something so simple that I would miss most. Mother made the most perfect bread and her jam was quite simply heavenly.'

'Aw, stop,' groaned Albie. 'Now you're making me even more hungry.'

'What about some lovely beef casserole,' Jellicoe teased. 'With those heavy dumpling things you British seem to love so much?'

'Stoooop,' said Albie with his tongue hanging out.

'What food do you miss most from home?' I asked Jellicoe.

'Jerk chicken,' sighed Jellicoe. 'Goat curry...mmmmm. And of course ackee and saltfish.'

'What's ackee when it's at home?' Albie asked.

'Ackee my friend is the food of Heaven,' Jellicoe smiled. 'A fruit from the Gods.'

'Bet it wouldn't beat good old fish and chips,' said Albie.

Jellicoe said nothing but raised an eyebrow and sighed deeply.

* * *

Waiting for news of the convoy was far worse than waiting for Christmas to come when I was a boy. The promise of food and relief was tantalising but it came with the knowledge that men would die as they tried to get it to us.

We knew the ships were being attacked. It had been inevitable when they set out on their mission. What we didn't know was the extent of the damage.

'It's the most protected convoy of the war so I heard,' said Albie. 'They've armour-plated the ships and kitted them out with anti-aircraft guns. The big tanker with all our fuel is being protected by destroyers and there are carriers with Spitfires ready to take to the air if Hitler and Mussolini send trouble from the skies.'

As the days ticked by and the convoy came ever closer to us, the stories of destruction and loss filtered through to us waiting on Malta. The losses were immense despite the protection. HMS Eagle, the carrier with the Spitfires aboard, was torpedoed by an Italian submarine. It tipped on its side and the planes slid into the water before the ship followed it, all headed for the bottom of the sea.

'I feel so helpless,' said Jellicoe. 'They're too far away for us to get to still.'

Hundreds of planes were sent to bombard the convoy and many of the ships carrying supplies were lost, along with hundreds of incredibly brave people who'd risked everything to try and save Malta. Jellicoe was right, it was terrible knowing what was going on and not being able to do anything to help.

As the ships came closer to Malta we could hear the ferocity of the attacks well before we could see the ships. Far in the distance we could see towering plumes of black smoke and finally we saw the ships. Little smudges on the horizon, with the occasional burst of fire as one of them was hit.

On 13th August, what was left of the convoy was close enough for our Spitfires to leave the island and help defend.

'We're being scrambled,' Jellicoe told me. 'The bloody Italian Regia Marina are sending another fleet to attack. The Air Vice Marshall has ordered us into the air to give them what for.'

The Regia Marina, the Italian navy, had fast boats and we knew they could do a lot of damage. Our navy would be out to defend no doubt, but they'd need all the help we could offer.

I kitted up and took to the skies, grateful in a strange way that I was able to play a part in bringing the remaining ships safely to Malta.

'Right men,' said our pilot, Squadron Leader Bert Hayward. 'It looks as though the Luftwaffe are easing off now they've taken out so many of our ships. They're leaving it to the blasted Italians on the sea. But they're strong and fast and packed with weapons and I'm afraid if we take these chaps on with just the manpower we have on the island we won't stand a chance.'

My heart chilled at these words.

'However, the Vice Marshall has a plan to bluff Mussolini and his merry band of seamen. We are going to fly over and give those Italians all we can from the Wellingtons. But more importantly we are going to make them think a massive allied attack is on the way. Hopefully those mummy's boys will turn tail if they think they're in for a big assault.'

'Will it work, Sir?' I asked.

'It better had,' said the Squadron Leader.

* * *

From the sky I looked down on a ship named HMS Rochester Castle, still a way from the island and being attacked by Italian and German bombers. I found out later that she was the first of the convoy to successfully make it through to the Harbour.

'Target sighted,' said Sergeant Sam Wallace from the nose.

I clicked frantically away in Morse Code and waited for a reply from shore.

'Sir, they're informing me we have backup on the way,' I informed him. 'The U.S Air Force are sending a fleet of aircraft to help liberate.'

'Let's hope the enemy have heard that too,' he said. 'It's all nonsense of course. Nobody else is coming to help us.'

For the first time since I had become a telegraphist, I crossed my fingers and prayed that our messages were being intercepted.

The Morse clicked with a new message.

'Sir, we're being told to drop illuminating flares,' I called. 'To show those non-existent American's where we are.'

'Right you are,' said the Squadron Leader.

The darkening evening sky, already lit by gun fire and bombs was suddenly flooded with new light as the flairs exploded.

'Sir, they're turning round,' shouted Wallace.

'Good show,' cheered Jellicoe. 'We bluffed them.'

And we had. The Regia Marina stood down and were retreating, convinced that a massive threat was about to hit them.

We flew back to the island and over the HMS Brsibane Star as she also came into port.

With four ships safely docked at Grand Harbour, we were allowed time to rest. I was exhausted but only slept for a few hours before reporting for duty.

'Go to the Harbour,' said the Squadron Leader. The Spitfires are bringing in the SS Ohio. I'm afraid she's the last one remaining of the convoy.

'The others?' I asked.

He just shook his head. Of fourteen ships only four had made it and the Ohio would make it five.

'All hands are needed to unload supplies. If you hurry, you'll be able to jump on board a truck leaving in...' he checked his watch, 'precisely five minutes.'

I made sure I was on that truck. If I could be no more use in the air that day then I wanted to help in any way I could.'

The sight that met us at Grand Harbour was like nothing I had ever seen before. It was evening but the place was thrumming with activity. Crates being unloaded, officials directing supplies to be stored and those that were to be sorted for immediate distribution.

The SS Ohio, with the help of three destroyers and an air full of Spitfires could be seen approaching the harbour at a terrifyingly slow rate. So slow that it looked as though it wasn't even moving.

I made my way down to the Harbour's edge to find out how I could best be put to use.

'John?' a voice behind me said. The voice made me stand still. I didn't turn because I was sure that my mind was playing a horrendous trick on me. I carried on down towards the docks but a hand on my shoulder stopped me. I shut my eyes, not daring to turn around and find out that the truth I so desperately hoped for was indeed a trick.

'John, John Hallett,' said the voice, cracking with emotion. 'It IS you!'

I finally turned and there standing before me was Bill.

CHAPTER 21

When Eliza read about the miracle of Bill's appearance, she sat up in bed.

'Everything alright, Darling?' Ganny asked from the bed next to her.

'Bill's alive!' said Eliza.

'Ah,' said Ganny. 'One of the few wonderful twists the war gave us.'

'Why didn't you tell me?' Eliza said.

'I wanted you to feel a little of John's sadness,' Ganny said. 'Just a little. That way the joy and surprise of finding him standing on the Harbour would be so much more precious.'

Eliza hugged the journal to her.

'I like sharing a room with you,' she said.

'I have to say that I do as well,' said Ganny. 'Mrs Cox really is very kind to let us stay. It's sort of like a mini adventure. And now we know Mum is going to be completely fine and so will the house after the chaps with the machines come in tomorrow and start the big clean up job, I think we are allowed to enjoy our adventure just a little bit.'

It was a strange sort of adventure, but then that was Ganny all over. She always found a way to make the best out of everything.

* * *

They spent just over a week at Mrs Cox's house and the summer holidays were very close to ending by the time they were finally allowed to go back home.

'What's the house like now?' Jonno asked as he and Eliza walked over the golf course.

'It all stinks,' said Eliza. 'Smoky and then cleaning chemicals too.'

'Yuck!' said Jonno.

'And the kitchen is disgusting,' said Eliza. 'But it's being stripped out next week and Mum has been busy picking out a new one.'

'I thought she was supposed to be resting,' said Jonno.

'She is,' said Eliza. 'But she says hospital is boring and she needs something to keep her mind busy because Dad has banned her from working.'

'When will she come home?'

'Tomorrow,' said Eliza. 'But she's going to have to go back in again to have new skin put over the worst patch on her arm. She's lucky though, because she can still use her arm and hand, it's just the skin that was damaged.'

'Well, you know one good thing about this fire business,' said Jonno.

'What?'

'Ganny rescued your Mum and helped save her arm. Sounds like she also stopped the fire spreading and wrecking the rest of the house,' said Jonno. 'No way they can pack her off now.'

* * *

That evening Dad was sitting in the garden reading a book. He hadn't exactly stopped working since the fire but he was definitely doing a lot less. He went to the hospital every day and was around more in the evenings too.

'Dad,' said Eliza. 'You know how Ganny saved everything. With Mum I mean, and the house.'

'She has always been more than a bit special,' Dad said. 'But I still cannot believe what she managed to do. Where she found the strength and courage I'll never know.'

'I think it was living in the war and working with her dad and the Home Guard.'

'Do you know, I think you're probably right,' said Dad.

'That's definitely how she knew what to do in the fire and how to look after Mum's burns,' said Eliza. 'So, she's a very useful and brilliant sort of person to have around.'

'Ah,' said Dad. 'I think I know where you're going with this.'

'I'm just saying that surely now you won't make her go into a care home.'

'Sweetheart, have you actually talked to Ganny about this?' Dad asked. 'Have you asked her what she wants?'

'I don't need to,' said Eliza. 'I know she wants to stay with us. Why would she want to go into a stupid old people's home when she has a home of her own and a family who loves her and needs her?'

Dad put his arm around Eliza and kissed her on the head.

'Just go and have a chat with her,' said Dad. 'And if she wants to stay with us then of course she can.'

Eliza felt her whole self fizzing with excitement and relief. Ganny could stay!

Ganny was already in bed when Eliza went up to see her.

'Mum is coming home tomorrow,' said Ganny. 'That's exciting.'

'Yes,' said Eliza. 'I just hope we can keep her away from work for a bit.'

'I think you might find things are a little bit different from now on,' said Ganny. 'Big events like this have a way of making people take a good long look at their choices.'

'Maybe,' said Eliza. 'Ganny, you love living with us don't you?'

'I do,' said Ganny. 'Seeing your smiling face each day makes me happier than I can begin to tell you.'

'I knew it,' said Eliza, bending down to give Ganny a hug.

'Climb aboard Darling,' said Ganny, patting the bed next to her. 'I do need to tell you something.'

Eliza sat down and tried not to let the wobble in her tummy take over. She didn't know what Ganny was going to say. It might be something brilliant.

'Darling, I'm a pretty ancient old thing these days and my legs don't always work as well as I'd like them to,' Ganny said. 'Especially since the fire.'

'But I can help you,' said Eliza.

'And you do a fabulous job of it. But you'll be back at school soon and I get terribly lonely on my own so I asked your Dad to have a look for somewhere else for me to live.'

Eliza stood up in disbelief.

'You asked him?' she said.

'I did,' said Ganny. 'Just to see what the choices were. He has found a very lovely place and they have a space for me.'

'No,' said Eliza. 'Please Ganny.'

'It's very close,' said Ganny. 'In fact, you could even walk there from your school so you can come and visit me as often as you like. We can play Backgammon and have char and chat time. All the things we love. But I'll have people around during the day that I can talk to and there are carers who can help me if I take a tumble.'

Eliza didn't know what to think. She knew she was being selfish but the thought of no more Ganny at home was a terrible one.

'I don't want you to go,' she said quietly.

'I know you don't Poppet,' said Ganny. 'And it makes me sad to see you sad. But we'll both get used to it very quickly I promise. And you'll soon make so many wonderful new friends at school that you won't even want to come and see me.'

Eliza snuggled up to Ganny and breathed in her smell of lavender and chocolate biscuits. 'That won't ever happen,' she said.

CHAPTER 22

MALTA – SEPTEMBER 1942

At around 8am on August 15th – the Feast of Santa Marija – the tanker SS Ohio finally docked in Grand Harbour. Battered and bruised but still buoyant and full of the fuel needed to keep the RAF in the skies and protecting Malta.

The response from the people watching assembled was magical to watch. There was singing, cheering, clapping and crying. People threw their hats into the air whilst others waved handkerchiefs.

And right in the middle were Bill and I. Cheering and waving and singing with all our hearts. Looking at each other now and again because neither of us could quite believe that fate had brought us back together. I patted my pocket. Perhaps Susan Rabbit had been at work again.

* * *

After the horrendous ordeal of Operation Pedestal, Bill was given leave of absence for a couple of days before he was due to report back for duty.

'You've been having a fine old war,' I said. 'I thought you joined the King's good old Royal Navy for an easy life of operating radios.'

Bill's smile was watery. 'Chance would be a fine thing,' he said. 'But I'm still alive by some miracle.'

'And an even greater miracle that you're here,' I said. 'I still can't believe it.'

* * *

I took Bill to the farm and we met Maurice out at the front. He shook Bill's hand firmly and gave him one of his very best toothless grins.

'Hello,' Maurice said. 'How are you?'

'Very well thank you Sir,' said Bill. 'It's most awfully kind of you to have me. What a simply marvellous farm you have here.'

Maurice looked at him in confusion.

'He doesn't really speak English,' I explained. 'Just a few words and phrases that I've taught him.'

'John,' said Azalea. Coming around the side of the farmhouse with Abigail attached to her hip as always.

'Azalea,' I said. 'I'd like you to meet my very good friend Bill Chandler.'

Bill flushed red, not unusual for him. But when I looked at Azalea I saw that she too was flushing.

'Very nice to meet you,' said Bill, offering his hand.

Her eyes didn't leave his as she took it. And I think it's

very safe to say that that was the exact moment Bill and Azalea fell in love.

* * *

Later that evening, back in the mess at Luqa, I introduced Bill to Jellicoe and Albie.

'One of our saviours,' Jellicoe said. 'We owe so very much to you and the rest of the crews in the operation.'

We shared a moment of silence as we thought about the men lost to Operation Pedestal.

'John says you're a radio operator,' said Albie.

'That's right,' said Bill. 'Like John, I gather. I can't tell you what a weight off my mind it is to find out he didn't make it as a pilot.'

Bill chuckled.

'Hang on a minute there,' I said.

'It's been my biggest worry of the war that they'd let you behind the controls of a fighter plane.'

He held his arms out as wings like we used to as children and made the noise of an engine.'

'Instead, I took a leaf out of your book,' I said.

'I told you Morse Code would come in useful,' John smiled.

'I remember the day John received the letter that told him you were missing,' Jellicoe said. 'He was distraught.'

'I wouldn't go that far,' I joked. 'A little put out perhaps but hardly distraught.'

'That's not true,' said Jellicoe. 'You said you had a huge regret and that you'd never be able to make it better.'

Bill looked at me and I opened my mouth to speak but he held up his hand and shook his head.

'No don't,' he said. 'It's all past and forgotten.'

'And what we all really want to talk about is how you came back from the dead, old boy,' said Albie, as subtle as ever.

Bill's story was a brave one. He told us how his boat had indeed been sunk off the coast of France but that he'd been picked up almost a whole day later by a French fishing boat.

'I was freezing cold and pretty much unconscious,' he said. 'Another hour and I think all they'd have found was a rather attractive body.'

I nudged him at this point and we both smiled.

'Well, I recovered and rejoined my brigade. We got sent to Scotland and were told about this rather important mission to Malta of all places. We weren't given any details until we were on the Brisbane Star. The Captain told us of the dangers and we were given the opportunity to disembark, although we'd have had to stay in a detention centre until the end of the mission to stop us spilling the beans. It was that secret. But not one man got off the ship. We all decided to take our chances and come over here to save your sorry souls.'

'And very grateful we all are for that,' said Jellicoe.

'Amen,' I agreed.

* * *

Bill was granted a transfer and the right to stay on Malta as a naval telegraphist at Lascaris. He had become incredibly quick and talented at Morse Code and so his transfer was readily agreed.

He told me that this decision was so we could make up for lost time but I knew there was another much more attractive reason calling him to stay on the Fortress Island.

I wasn't sure whether the bond that was forged between Bill and Azalea was so strong because of the impact of the war or whether they simply found that rarest of things. True love. Either way, when he had days off, it wasn't me he came to visit.

Life on Malta became easier for us all. The food and medical supplies certainly helped but the fuel needed to step up the RAF and naval defence of the island was even more valuable in a way as it meant the raids became less.

The last time I saw Bill and Azalea was on September 21st. After a year and a half, my squadron was leaving the island so I went to say goodbye.

'You will be back?' Azalea asked.

'Of course I will,' I said. 'We're being sent to North Africa for a few weeks. They need help with those blasted oil tankers the Germans keep trying to get across to their men and then there's talk of leave. I think we might even get to see England again but I'll be back and who knows, it might even be in a time of peace.'

Azalea gave me such a big hug that I felt my newly fixed ribs and lung struggle a little.

Maurice clapped me hard on the back and said something to me in Maltese.

'He wishes you luck,' said Azalea.

For the first time since we'd pulled her out of the rubble of the church, Abigail looked at my face. Then she held out both hands, asking to be picked up. When I did, she buried her head into my shoulder and I am sure she whispered 'John' (or at least her version of it) into my hair.

I breathed her in and wondered just how long it would be before I saw her again. How much would she have grown and would she even recognise me.

'Here,' I said, taking Susan Rabbit from my pocket. 'She's called Susan and she will bring you luck and keep you safe until the war is over. Kiss her nose every day for me.'

I demonstrated what I meant with a little kiss on Susan's nose. Abigail copied me and then stretched up to kiss my nose too.

'I think you've got a fan,' said Bill.

I smiled as I passed Abigail back to Azalea.

'Look after them,' I said.

Bill nodded. 'See you very soon,' he said.

As we went to shake hands, I found myself pulling him into a hug.

I stopped to wave as I turned out of the farm. Bill had his arm around Azalea and it cheered me to see how happy my friends were after all the hardships they'd seen. I took the photo from my pocket. The one of my family standing by the sandbags back at home.

'I think we're all going to be alright you know,' I whispered to them. 'And I might even get to see my own family really soon.'

I kissed the photo, tucked it back into my pocket and whistled quietly to myself as I walked down the road back toward Valletta.

CHAPTER 23

That night, Eliza felt glummer than ever before. Ganny was leaving, Anaya was leaving, Jonno and Scout would be going back to Manchester soon as he was only staying for the summer and the summer was nearly over.

She lay on her bed and cried as though her heart had been broken with a sledgehammer. Once the tears finally stopped, she rolled over and hugged Alfie Bear to her. Eliza was exhausted but her eyes wouldn't stay shut when she tried to sleep. The more she tried not to think of all the people about to leave her, the more her horrid brain forced her to remember. In the end, she picked up Ganny's notebook and read until the last page. She turned over, hoping for more but there was nothing. She was left empty, desperate to know the ending but sad when she remembered that, for John at least, that ending was not to be a happy one.

* * *

As soon as she woke up, Eliza went to find Ganny who was downstairs in her dressing gown, sitting in her favourite spot on the sofa with Boo on her lap.

'What happened to them all?' Eliza said. 'It isn't finished.'

'You reached the end of John's story,' said Ganny. 'Now then, I can answer some of your questions. But some I just don't know. I wish I did. I will start with the happiest news. Bill and Azalea married right at the end of the war.'

'Yes!' said Eliza. 'I thought they would.'

'Bill stayed in Malta with Azalea and took on the farm after the war ended. They came to visit a few times when we still lived near Bill's parents. Although we missed John dreadfully, it was wonderful to see Bill and Azalea and to hear their stories about John's time on Malta. We met little Abigail and watched her grow. They really were the happiest and loveliest of families. I have photos in a box upstairs. I'll show you. Azalea wrote with a new photo of Abigail every year and carried on writing until she died almost fifteen years ago now. Just one year after Bill.'

'What about Abigail?'

'Abigail grew up and had a family of her own. She still lives on Maurice's farm and we write to each other every Christmas. Why don't we send her a letter? She knows all about you and I'm sure she'd love to hear from you.'

'I'd really like that,' said Eliza. It seemed incredible that the little girl she'd just been reading about was now an old lady in her eighties. It would be brilliant if she was able to get in touch with her and ask more questions about Bill and Azalea. She also wanted to know how Malta recovered after the war finally left it alone.

'And then there was John,' said Ganny with a sigh. 'My

tricky, funny, handsome, kind-hearted big brother. As you will have read, he was sent across the sea to North Africa. He set off in a Wellington bomber on September 22nd 1942 but the plane never got as far as Africa. Poor John has no memory of anything after take-off that day but his plane went down somewhere along the way, almost certainly due to engine failure of some sort. It was frighteningly common for these things to happen. All six men on board were counted as missing and that was it, six more lives lost and six more families grieving. Just like that.'

'He shouldn't have given Susan Rabbit away,' Eliza said. 'He gave away all his good luck.'

'I sometimes wonder about that too,' said Ganny. 'But do you know what I think?'

Eliza shook her head.

'I think that if he did give away his luck, he gave it to Abigail and Azalea and Bill. And I like to think that just maybe Susan Rabbit and John are the reason they all survived in the end.'

Eliza saw the corners of Ganny's crinkled eyes spark with tears. She followed Ganny's gaze and looked hard at the empty chair. Was she imagining it or was there the very faint outline of someone sitting in it? She blinked and looked again. The outline seemed to be getting clearer as she looked. It began filling out and making sense.

'John?' Eliza whispered.

The young man in the smart RAF uniform now sitting in the chair, as clear as her own hands, smiled at her. It was a smile she knew so well. It was Ganny's smile.

'She sees me at last!' John said.

'I told you she would,' said Ganny. 'When she was ready.'

'I can't believe it,' said Eliza. She couldn't help staring at the man, her great-great-uncle John.

'You read my story then,' he said.

'Yes,' she managed to say.

'We made a funny bunch, didn't we?' he laughed. 'I think I met some of the very best people on our planet whilst I was in Malta. Such courage and strength. It's little wonder the King gave the whole island a medal, is it?'

'No,' said Eliza.

'You look a bit shocked,' said Ganny.

'You were telling the truth,' said Eliza. 'Oh Ganny, I'm sorry I didn't believe you.'

'I can't say I blame you,' said John, showing off his wide smile again. 'Liffy was always good at telling tall stories.'

'Not this time,' said Ganny, and Eliza thought she'd never seen her looking happier.

'What happened to the others?' Eliza asked. 'Did Jellicoe survive?'

'I wish I knew,' John said. 'Jellicoe was headed for Africa with me in a different plane. I don't know if he made the journey. I know Albie stayed on Malta after we left but I wish I knew what happened after that.'

'We could use the internet to find out,' said Eliza. 'I'm sure we could find something if you've got their full names.'

'The what?' John asked.

'The internet,' said Ganny. 'You'd love it, it's frightfully clever. You ask it anything you want and it gives you the answer.'

'Good heavens,' said John. 'That would be rather wonderful if you could find out. I bet that nice Jonno chap would help you.'

Eliza thought back to the day Jonno had been round and they'd stayed in the garden.

'He could see you, couldn't he?' Eliza said.

'Some people are more open to ghosts than others,' Ganny said. 'Dogs too. Boo here has been a fan of John ever since they first met.'

'Goodness,' said Eliza jumping up suddenly. 'Jonno! I completely forgot. I'm supposed to be meeting him in the park in ten minutes. Uncle John, will you be here when I get back? I've got so much I want to ask you.'

John smiled. 'I'm not going anywhere in a hurry. Now off you go and say hello to Jonno for me.'

* * *

'So, you can finally see him then,' said Jonno.

'It was so weird,' said Eliza. 'One minute the chair was empty and the next... there he was!'

'I told you to keep an open mind.'

'Ganny says that ghosts only appear to people who need them,' said Eliza. 'Ganny saw John when she was lonely and I saw him when I needed answers to all the questions I had. But why did you need him?'

Jonno shrugged. 'Who knows?' he said.

Eliza wanted to go round to Jonno's house to meet his Grandma but the one time she'd asked him, he'd fobbed her with an excuse and she hadn't tried again.

'Do you want to come back to mine?' Eliza said instead. 'The fire smell's almost gone and I know Ganny and John would like to see you. You can help me on the internet. I'm going to try and find out what happened to Jellicoe and Albie.'

'Isn't your Mum coming home from hospital this afternoon?' Jonno asked.

'Yeah, but she won't mind,' said Eliza. 'Probably won't even notice.'

'I think I won't this time. You should be with your family. But another time would be cool.'

'When are you going back to Manchester?' Eliza said.

'Dunno,' said Jonno. 'I never really know until it happens.'

* * *

When Eliza got home, Dad had already picked Mum up from hospital and she was sitting on the sofa next to Ganny. Her arm was bandaged up and her leg had a big dressing stuck on it but she looked pretty good apart from that. John's chair was empty and Eliza wondered if he had left or if she just couldn't see him right then. Mum and Ganny were laughing about something and Mum looked relaxed. Something Eliza didn't think she'd seen since Mum's new job had snatched her away.

'Eliza,' said Mum. 'I've missed you. Come and sit down, just watch the arm.'

'Hi Mum,' said Eliza. 'How are you feeling?'

'Much better for being out of that hospital I can tell you. The staff were amazing, but it's so good to be home. Eliza, I wanted to say that I'm really sorry.'

'Sorry?' said Eliza. 'What for?'

'Well apart from burning down the house, sorry for not being there for you more. Whilst you were out Ganny has been telling me a few things about what your life has been like lately and I can't believe you had so much going on without me knowing about it.'

'Don't be cross, Darling,' said Ganny. 'I thought she should know because she's your mother and she cares so much about you.'

'Things are going to change round here,' said Mum. 'Starting with work. I'm going to take a proper break to get myself better and to look after you and be here for you when you start your new school. And when I do go back, I'm going to tell them that you are my number one priority and that I won't be working weekends or late into the evening anymore.'

'Really?' said Eliza.

'Really,' said Mum. 'And I'm going to find someone who can help us as well. Someone for you to speak to about your worries and who can help you understand them a bit better so they're easier to cope with.'

'I'm not sure I need to see someone like that,' said Eliza, suddenly panicking at the thought of a person she didn't know poking and prying into her secrets.

'One step at a time I think Poppet,' said Ganny.

It felt good to sit there with her family that evening. All phones were left in another room and Dad ordered Chinese take away, which they all ate with chopsticks; even Ganny who'd never used them before but refused to eat with a fork when there was something new to try and learn. Mum slurped a big mouthful of noodles and made everyone laugh.

'What?' she said. 'I'm learning to be one handed.'

'When it comes to chopsticks, we're all one handed,' Dad said.

At some point, whilst they all snuggled in to watch a film

together, John came back to his chair and Boo went straight over to sit at his feet.

Eliza smiled at him across the room. And John winked back.

CHAPTER 24

'Where are you heading?' Mum asked as Eliza laced up her trainers.

'I'm taking Boo for a walk,' she replied.

'Lovely,' said Mum. 'You do stick to the park and golf course, don't you?'

'Ummm,' said Eliza, not looking at her Mum.

'Eliza, it's important.'

'It's okay,' said Eliza. 'I just go into the woods with my friend Jonno. We've been going in all summer and it's been fine.'

'I just want you to stay safe,' Mum said. 'There are dangerous parts of the woods.'

'It's fine,' said Eliza again. 'We're careful I promise.'

'If you're old enough to be going into the woods then you're old enough to hear about a very sad thing that happened there when you were about one,' said Mum. 'A young boy who was down from Manchester, staying with his Gran for the summer was walking his dog on his own in the woods.'

Eliza stopped dead and started listening.

'He was by the chalk quarry pit when the dog started chasing rabbits. Anyway, he ended up chasing one right over the edge of the quarry and the boy ran after him. The chalk up there is so flaky and it had been raining. It gave way and that poor boy was found at the bottom of the quarry pit. I remember it so well, it was awful. He'd hit his head hard on the rocks and they never managed to wake him up.

'Jonno?' Eliza whispered.

'I think he was called Jonathan actually,' Mum said. 'His Gran was a friend of Mrs Cox's. Why? Have you heard the story already?'

'I've got to go,' said Eliza.

'I mean it Eliza,' said Mum. 'Be careful. And please don't go into the woods.'

* * *

Eliza ran all the way to the park, surprising Boo who bounded along next to her on his lead.

'Are you the same Jonathan who fell down the chalk pit?' she puffed when she got there.

'What?' said Jonno.

'It is you, isn't is?' Eliza said. 'That's why you could see John and why you never drink anything or eat anything. It's why the cobwebs never rub away when you touch them and why the den was so overgrown and rotten, because you didn't make it last year. You made it ten years ago when you came to visit your Gran. It's why you haven't changed your clothes once in all the time I've known you and why you wear that green jumper even though it's been hot every day.'

'Eliza, slow down.'

'It's why Dad couldn't see you when you came round but Ganny could because she knew what to look for. It's why you told me I should be open minded about ghosts,' she said. 'Because you are one.'

'Wow,' said Jonno. 'I wondered if you'd figure it out.'

'So, it's true?'

'Pretty much,' said Jonno.

Eliza had run out of things to say so she just stared at the ground.

'Does it matter?' said Jonno.

She thought about it. Did it matter... really? At the beginning of the summer she'd been miserable about Ganny and Anaya and petrified of going to the new school. And then she'd met Jonno. Right when she needed a friend the most. He'd helped her in so many ways and she felt better about almost everything that had been troubling her just those few weeks earlier.

'No,' she said. 'I don't think it does. I just wanted to know.'

* * *

There were just three days left of the summer holidays and it was the afternoon before Ganny was due to move into her care home. She and Eliza were outside, sitting under the sunshade with John. As always seemed to happen these days, Boo was curled up fast asleep at John's feet.

'Jonno and I have been doing some research online,' said Eliza, proudly. 'There's loads out there if you know where to look, especially when you've got so much background information to help you.'

She looked at John when she said this.

'Glad I could be of service,' John said.

'What did you discover?' Ganny asked.

'Jellicoe survived,' Eliza told them. 'He went back to Jamaica and lived there for the rest of his life. I even found some photos of him.'

She passed over the laptop for Ganny to see. John leaned over her shoulder.

'Good gracious,' he said. 'There he is. Flying Officer Jellicoe Hyde, so he did get promoted after all. What about Albie?'

'He wasn't so lucky,' Eliza said. 'He was on an aircraft carrier going back to England when it hit a mine.'

'Poor Albie,' said John. 'But I'm glad to know. Thank you, Eliza.'

Just then the doorbell rang and Eliza heard Mum go to answer it.

'Eliza,' she called. 'It's for you.'

Eliza looked at Ganny in surprise.

'Go on,' said Ganny.

'Anaya!' Eliza screamed when she saw her friend. She ran towards her and gave her the biggest hug she'd ever given anyone.

'I wanted to talk to you,' Eliza said. 'I wanted to say sorry but I didn't see your message and then I went round but you'd already left.'

'I missed you,' said Anaya. 'I was going to call a couple of times from Amma's phone but I didn't know what you'd say and I didn't want to have another row when there was so much distance between us.'

Eliza hugged her again. 'I missed you too and I'm really

sorry. It's going to be rubbish at Highmoor Comp without you. But I know how much dancing means to you and I get why you have to take your chances when they're given. And we can still meet up in the holidays can't we?'

'Of course we can Elz,' said Anaya. 'And Nottingham isn't like India. I can have my phone on so we can talk to each other every day.'

* * *

The last days of the summer passed in a blur. Eliza was so busy catching up with Anaya, walking with Jonno and helping Ganny settle her things into her sunny room at the care home that she hardly had any time to worry about the first day of school until it arrived.

She sat at the breakfast table with a knot in her stomach that made eating anything almost impossible.

'Just a little bit of toast,' Mum said.

'I think I'll be sick,' said Eliza.

'Here,' said Dad, passing her a bar of fruit and nut chocolate. 'Put that in your bag in case you feel hungry later.

'What?' he said, catching Mum's eye. 'Just this once, because it's our baby's first day.'

'Are you sure we can't drive you?' Mum said.

'Stop fussing,' said Eliza. 'I don't want to be the only one whose parents take me. I'll never make friends that way.'

'No,' said Mum. 'Right. Well at least let us take you to the bus stop. We've both cleared our diaries this morning specially.'

'Just as far as the corner then,' said Eliza. 'But not all the way. I don't want everyone to see me.'

Eliza put her new creaky leather shoes on and tied up the laces. They were so new and shiny she'd have to find some dirt on the way to rub into them. Her new blazer was itchy on her skin and the fresh white shirt felt a bit too white. She looked in the mirror and suddenly wished she hadn't gone for plaits. What if nobody else had plaits and she looked like a stupid primary school girl.

'The postie is early today,' said Dad, picking up the bundle of letters that had just plopped onto the mat. 'There's one for you Fizzy Lizzy. Looks like it's come from Malta.'

Eliza grabbed the thick envelope and ripped it open. Inside was a long letter but she didn't have time to read it before school. She flicked to the end and read out the signature.

'It's from Abigail,' she said in delight. 'Uncle John's friend. I wrote to her last week and Ganny gave me the address. She must have written back straight away.'

'You'd better save it for later,' said Dad. 'Or you'll miss the bus.'

'I'll take it to school with me,' said Eliza. 'I'm going straight round to see Ganny after school so we can read it together.'

'Lovely thought,' said Mum.

Eliza tried to stuff the letter back into the envelope but something stopped it. She shook out the envelope and a tiny rabbit fell into her hand. She was made from well-worn brown velvet and was wearing a little floral dress.

'What on earth is that?' Dad asked.

'Susan Rabbit,' said Eliza, kissing the tip of her nose and tucking her and the letter into her inside blazer pocket.

* * *

Eliza stopped at the corner and stooped down to give Boo a massive hug. Then she hugged Mum and Dad tightly.

'Good luck my baby,' said Mum.

'Knock 'em dead Fizzy Lizzy,' said Dad. 'I'm so proud of you.'

The butterflies in her stomach jumped and swooped as she left her family behind and walked down the road to the bus stop. There was already a bunch of kids wearing the same uniform as she was but she didn't recognise anyone.

When the bus arrived, she waited until everyone else got on and then she climbed up the steps and found a seat by the window. She could feel the little lump next to her heart where Susan Rabbit lay and she felt a little calmer. Not brave, not quite yet, but definitely calmer.

'Can I sit here?' asked a girl wearing the same uniform as Eliza.

'Sure,' said Eliza, moving her bag to let the girl sit.

Eliza looked back at Mum, Dad and Boo and they waved at her.

'Is that your mum and dad?' the girl next to her said.

'It's ok, mine are hiding around the next corner. Parents can be so embarrassing. Oh wow, is that your Jack Russell?'

'That's Boo,' she said.

'I love Jack Russells,' said the girl. 'I have one too, he's called Tombo. Maybe we could take them for a walk one day. I'm Lily by the way.'

As the bus began to move off, Eliza looked back again.

Mum, Dad and Boo were still there. But they weren't the only ones on the corner now. Standing next to them, waving wildly were Jonno and Uncle John.

Eliza waved back and felt just a tiny bit braver.

'I'm Eliza,' she said. 'Tombo sounds great. I'm sure he and Boo would get on brilliantly.'

AUTHOR'S NOTE

This book couldn't have been written without research. Whilst many of the events in John's story happened and I have tried to be as thorough as I can with my fact finding, please forgive any discrepancies where I have fallen short.

It may seem as though parts of this story are a little far-fetched and things couldn't possibly have been as bad on Malta as John found them. But on April 15th 1942 the entire island really did receive the George Cross medal for braveness (it was announced two days later in The Times of Malta) and there was very good reason for this.

The location of Malta made it strategically vital and because of this it was both heavily attacked and ferociously defended. In 1941 and 1942 it was the most bombed place on Earth with over 3000 bombs dropping, wiping out almost all towns and cities and killing around 1,500 civilians and many Allied servicemen. It was thanks to the protection of the network of limestone tunnels and caves that more lives weren't lost.

The story about the buried crypt beneath the church is sadly true. According to Joseph, an eyewitness, only one little girl was saved. I couldn't find the name of the church so I chose to name it after Santa Marija.

By the time Operation Pedestal brought much needed supplies to Malta, they were only a few weeks away from surrender. Without fuel, food and other essential supplies, survival would have been impossible. Had this happened, then the war would almost certainly have been extended by one or even two years as Hitler, Germany and the AXIS troops took control of the Mediterranean and shipping routes to North Africa.

One fact I have twisted is Jellicoe's inclusion in this story. I can find no reference of black crewmen being sent to Malta but, once the colour ban was lifted at the beginning of the war, there were many brave people from the Caribbean who paid to cross the Atlantic and join the war effort. Whether or not any of them would have been stationed in Malta, it is an inclusion that I wanted to make so that we remember men like Warrant Officer James Hyde from Trinidad, killed when his Spitfire was shot down, and Officer John Jellicoe Blair who was an amazing navigator with the RAF and lived to see the end of the war – and the end of the century!

John and Elizabeth Hallett (Ganny) are the only characters in this book based on real people. Elizabeth was my Granny and, whilst she didn't claim to talk to John's ghost, she did keep his photograph and RAF cap in her room under a blue and white plaque of Mary and Jesus. Sadly, she didn't live as long as Ganny did, I wish she had as I'm sure she had plenty more stories to tell. It is my big regret that I didn't listen hard enough when she talked about John, and I didn't ask more questions whilst I still could.

John Hallett did go to Malta with 38th Squadron but the rest of this story is not based on his experiences. He wasn't in Malta long before he was sent across the sea in a Wellington Bomber. On September 22nd 1941 the plane went down and all six crewmen were lost:

Sgt Ronald Bateman – aged 20
Sgt John Charles Edwards-Cross – aged ?
Sgt Arthur John Brian Hallett – aged 19
Sgt Allen Francis Warner Moreas – aged ?
Sgt Elmer John Mutton – aged 24
Sgt Albert Richard Powell – aged 22

This book is to remember them and every man, woman and child who died on Malta or in the seas surrounding her.

RESEARCH ACKNOWLEDGEMENTS

BOOKS

Fortress Malta – An Island Under Siege 1940–1943 by James Holland.

185 The Malta Squadron by Anthony Rogers.

YOUTUBE

Tod Nicol's Outposts of Empire documentary.

Surviving The Siege of Malta by Breakthrough Entertainment.

James Holland's WWII The Siege of Malta documentary.

Pathe Newsreels.

TELEVISION AND FILM

Narrow Escapes of WWII – Operation Pedestal.

Malta Story.

WWW

The RAF Luqa Remembered website.

Warfare History article – Operation Pedestal: The Rescue of Malta, by Michael D. Hull.

If, like Eliza, you suffer from anxiety or depression and don't know where to turn or who to talk to then please know that you are not alone and there are things that can be done to help you. Try talking to a friend or an adult you trust. It doesn't have to be a parent, perhaps you have another family member who loves you as much as Ganny loves Eliza. Or maybe there's a teacher at your school who you think would listen and help. Don't be nervous, if you trust them then the adult you choose will undoubtedly be pleased you sought them out.

If there is nobody in your life you feel you can turn to, or you just feel happier talking to a stranger then there are people here for you too.

Childline.org.uk is a special charity for kids who need to talk. You can either e-mail them or give them a ring. Nobody will judge and nobody will force you to do something you're not ready to do. But they can support you and give you advice. It's what they're there for so please don't worry about getting in touch. You can also visit their website to safely and anonymously chat with other young people dealing with the same things as you.

ACKNOWLEDGEMENTS

My biggest and most humble thanks to my great uncle, John Hallett, and for every other person who died in the pursuit of peace. We owe you so much.

Thank you to my Granny, Elizabeth Hayter, who told me stories, showed me grainy photos and made sure we never forgot her beloved brother.

Thank you to the supremely talented writers, Tom Palmer and Lesley Parr for giving up your time to read early word docs and generously supplying me with such fantastic quotes.

As always, an ENORMOUS thanks to my writing partners and friends. Most especially to the Reading bunch who read early drafts of Wings – Clare, Donna, Fi and Meredith, you are incredible! To Jo Clark for your constant support and brunch dates and Jo Howard who went through Wings with a tooth comb.

To Emma Carroll and Liz Flanagan who were there at the very start of this journey and whose expert advice and feedback helped bring this story together.

To the Arvon girls for reading, supporting and zooming!

Sarah Horne, you are a genius. This is the most exquisite cover and I am so proud that our names share the same space. Thank you.

My stupendously wise agent, Amanda Preston, thank you for taking me on and allowing me to work on Wings whilst we prepare our new exciting project together. I can't wait to share that with the world.

A whopping thanks to Alex at Four Bears Books in Caversham for all your support and for stocking indie books when many don't.

To my family. Will, Lil, Mima, Mummy, Pa, Pip, Nick and Jon. I am so lucky to have your support always.

And lastly, to every single person who has read, reviewed or recommended any of my other books. It will always make my heart sing knowing that my stories are being heard.